Remember Josh.

Her dark gaze locked with his, her eyes hazy with desire and regret, and he figured he looked about the same. He wanted her, damn it, but there were good reasons for both of them to keep their distance, starting with Josh.

Then she sighed softly, and he thought to hell with Josh. All their lives, Joe had been the responsible, reliable, honorable twin, while Josh had done what he wanted, taken what he wanted and run when he wanted. Joe had always thought too much, and Josh hadn't thought at all.

At this moment Joe didn't want to think. He wanted to feel. To do.

Liz's breathing was shallow, ragged. Then he realized that it was his own echoing in his ears. She was hardly breathing at all, waiting, watching him, wanting…

Wanting him for who he was, or because he looked exactly like his brother?

Dear Reader,

I always fall in love with something when I write a book—a character, a place or something of importance to the story. This time there were those sweet sighs whenever Joe came onto the page, and Copper Lake is high on the list of places I'd like to live, but my true love affair was with coffee.

I'm a lifelong coffee nondrinker. But when I began a book about a man who owns a gourmet coffee shop, I thought the least I could do was sample some gourmet coffees. As luck would have it, at the same time I was doing this research, my niece came home from a year in El Salvador with bags of top Salvadoran coffee for everyone. One sip and I was in love. As further proof of serendipity, the only place to buy that coffee outside El Salvador was from the estate's only American roastery a mere twenty miles from my house.

It's fair to say that Liz fell in love with Joe over a cup of coffee. And so did I.

Marilyn Pappano

USA TODAY BESTSELLING AUTHOR

MARILYN PAPPANO

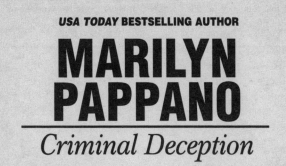

Criminal Deception

Romantic
SUSPENSE

 SILHOUETTE BOOKS

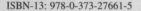

ISBN-13: 978-0-373-27661-5

Recycling programs
for this product may
not exist in your area.

CRIMINAL DECEPTION

Copyright © 2010 by Marilyn Pappano

This edition published by arrangement with Harlequin Books S.A.

® and TM are trademarks of Harlequin Books S.A., used under license.
Trademarks indicated with ® are registered in the United States Patent
and Trademark Office, the Canadian Trade Marks Office and in other
countries.

Visit Silhouette Books at www.eHarlequin.com

Printed in U.S.A.

Books by Marilyn Pappano

Silhouette Romantic Suspense

MARILYN PAPPANO

has spent most of her life growing into the person she was meant to be, but she isn't there yet. She's been blessed with family—her husband, their son, his lovely wife and a grandson who is almost certainly the most beautiful and talented baby in the world—and friends, along with a writing career that's made her one of the luckiest people around. Her passions, besides those already listed, include the pack of wild dogs who make their home in her house, fighting the good fight against the weeds that make up her yard, killing the creepy-crawlies that slither out of those weeds and, of course, anything having to do with books.

Chapter 1

Joe Saldana was a sucker for a pretty female, and he'd proven it twice in the past hour alone: he'd agreed to help Ellie Maricci with her new pet project, and with nothing more than an innocent look from Alyssa Lassiter's big blue eyes and a soft, "Pwease, Joe," he'd committed to help her father coach Little League this summer.

Now he sat in one corner of A Cuppa Joe, his Copper Lake, Georgia, coffee shop, gazing at his neighbor across the narrow table. Natalia Porter was unusually hesitant this afternoon, a sure sign that she wanted something from him. He was determined not to help her out by asking what.

She looked up from her afternoon grande mocha caffeine fix and casually said, "I went for a bike ride today."

"Huh." There was nothing unusual about that. Soon after moving into the cottage next door to his two months ago, she'd bought a bike and accompanied him on dozens of rides.

"I went out to Copper Lake."

"Huh." The lake for which the town was named was only three miles northeast of the square, a short ride for either of them.

"I found something." She gave up pretense for intensity that rushed out her words. "Two puppies. A male and a female. They're so cute and sweet and—and so hungry. They're nothing but skin and bones, and they kind of followed me home, but Mrs. Wyndham says I can't keep them. You, on the other hand, are so responsible and so reliable and just the perfect tenant, and if *you* wanted to keep them, why, of course that would be another matter entirely." Natalia paused for a breath, then looked at him hopefully. "So will you?"

He studied her. She was twenty-five, she'd told him, but with her ridiculously short brown hair and eyes that were way too big for her face, she looked about fifteen. Those eyes were green, at least for the day; she changed their color as often as she changed her contact lenses.

Very young, very innocent, very easy to say yes to.

Stubbornly, he didn't. "You know what puppies do? They pee all over everything. What they don't pee on, they chew up, and they eat like a horse. They'll tear my house apart the first time they're left alone. And in case you haven't noticed, with the hours I keep, they'd be alone a lot."

"I'll help with that," she said eagerly. "I'll take them out every two hours and I'll clean up whatever messes they make."

"I don't want pets."

"When was the last time you had one?"

"I don't have to have cancer to know I don't want it," he retorted. He was happy living by himself. He liked his shoes ungnawed on; he liked not sharing his bed. Being responsibility-free, except for the coffee shop, was his life's goal. The only thing he didn't want more than a puppy was two puppies.

Then he grinned faintly. That wasn't accurate. He didn't want to be audited by the IRS. He didn't want Starbucks to move into that empty space across the square. He didn't want global warming to be a fact, even though he believed it was.

He didn't want to ever see his brother again.

Oh, yeah, Josh trumped every other bad idea out there. Josh *was* the worst idea out there. Life would have been easier all around if he'd never been born.

Although how would that have affected Joe? After all, they'd come from the same egg.

And Joe had been dealing with him ever since.

"Please, Joe?"

"Look, Nat, I'll ask Miss Abigail—"

The bell over the door dinged and he glanced that way. For a moment, all he saw was red: a snug-fitting dress that hugged every curve it touched, from shoulder to breast to waist to hip. It was fire-engine, look-at-me red, and led to a pair of long tanned legs and high-heeled sandals, white dots on red and topped with a bow.

It was an amazing sight to a man with a fine appreciation for mile-long legs.

As the door *whooshed* shut and the newcomer took a few steps, curiosity raised his gaze. He'd been in Copper Lake a year and a half. How had he overlooked those legs before?

His glance slid back over those curves and skimmed across delicate features framed by sleek black curls before it clicked into one recognizable picture. All the appreciation disappeared, swallowed up whole by cold emptiness that spread instantly through him.

Slowly he got to his feet. Only dimly aware of Natalia's questioning look, he mumbled, "Yeah, okay, whatever," then crossed to the counter. He swore he felt the newcomer's gaze the instant it touched him, and he wondered in some distant part of his mind if she knew who he was, that he was Joe and not Josh.

Because last he heard, *she* had been Josh's.

She stopped near the cash register, where only two feet of marble separated them. She looked as cool as the stone between them, and elegant, too. Funny. Elegant had never been Josh's type.

But Josh had had no doubt that Elizabeth Dalton was exactly his type.

"Elizabeth." He drawled out all four syllables.

"I prefer Liz."

He'd heard those words before, the first time they'd met. Josh had introduced her as Beth, but she hadn't seemed at all like a Beth to him. She'd stated her preference that day, as now, but Josh had ignored her, and Joe… He hadn't called her anything. He'd been too busy keeping his tongue from hitting the floor.

"What brings you to Copper Lake?" Then the obvious answer to the question hit him and his gaze jerked toward the plate glass windows and the street beyond, searching for a glimpse of his brother. It would be just like him to send someone else in to smooth the way before he showed his face.

"I'm looking for Josh," Liz replied in that unruffled way of hers, and Joe's attention jerked again, back to her.

He couldn't decide which was more incredible—that his worthless brother had run out on a woman like Liz Dalton, that she thought he was worth tracking down, or that she thought he'd come to Joe. Even though they were identical twins, they'd been going their separate ways since they were about five years old. They hadn't been particularly close even before what had happened two years ago.

He picked up a spray bottle and a handful of towels, circled the counter to the nearest table, then started the task of scrubbing the top clean. "You're looking in the wrong town. This is the last place Josh would go if he's in trouble."

Liz followed him. "Then doesn't that make it the first place I should check?"

He wiped that table to a shine, then moved on to the next. Natalia, two tables away, wasn't even pretending that she wasn't listening to every word. "I haven't seen him in two years. I'm not sure I want to see him in the next twenty either."

"Has he called you?"

"Why would he do that?"

"To apologize?"

His laughter was more of a snort.

She shrugged, a silent acknowledgment that her suggestion was unlikely, then offered a better one. "To ask for money or help."

He rounded on her, moving closer, lowering his voice so Natalia would have to strain to hear. "Last time he asked me for anything, I damn near died. Do you really think he'd try again? Because if he did, I don't know whether I'd beat him to a pulp or let the people who tried to kill me do it instead."

Liz's eyes darkened a shade, and for a moment shock flashed there. He half expected her to chide, *You don't mean that,* but although her lips parted as if to speak, she remained silent.

Once more the bell above the door sounded, and he automatically looked that way as a group of girls wearing the tan-and-blue uniforms of the local middle school came in. There would be more behind them, followed in fifteen minutes by kids from the high school. As good an excuse as any to end this conversation.

"I've got customers. If you find Josh, tell him I said to go to hell and try not to take anyone with him." Stepping around her, he returned to the counter, washed his hands, forced a smile and went back to work.

* * *

"That went well," Liz murmured on the rush of a sigh. The words were meant just for her, but it was clear the girl at the nearest table heard them. Her startlingly emerald gaze met Liz's for an instant before she guiltily looked away.

Okay, so she hadn't expected Joe Saldana to be happy to see her or eager to discuss Josh. She'd just hoped he'd make her job easier. That he'd say, "Yeah, Josh is at the house. Go pick him up," or would at least know where he was or how to reach him.

Not that there'd been anything easy about Josh Saldana from the beginning.

She left the coffee shop, heading for her car parked around the corner. As she settled behind the wheel, she watched through the shop's side window while Joe joked with the girls lined up for drinks. He was old enough—just barely—to be their father, but that didn't stop at least three of them from gazing at him adoringly.

Granted, there was plenty to adore, on the outside, at least. He was over six feet tall, blond-haired and blue-eyed, tanned and lean. Liz could practically hear a Beach Boys' surfer tune playing in the background when she looked at him. He had a strong jaw, a straight nose, enough crook to his smile to give him a boyish look and enough sex appeal to give her a girlish tingle.

It had been there the first time they'd met—that sizzle— even though Josh had been standing between them, one arm draped possessively over her shoulder. She and Joe had exchanged looks and greetings, and something had sparked. And it had never fizzled out.

Well, maybe for him it had, she admitted as she started the engine. The last time she'd seen him, he was lying in an intensive-care bed, white as the sheet beneath him, hooked up to machines and IVs. His mother had quietly prayed and his father had wept, while Josh had been typically Josh. Nothing was ever his fault; he was always the innocent victim.

Liz had had her fill of victims like him.

The April afternoon was warm, but she opted for rolling the windows down instead of turning on the air conditioner. The breeze blew through her curls, and she drove with one hand on the wheel, the other holding them back from her face. Her destination was a mile or so away along quiet streets bordered by neatly kept houses, its drive marked by a small plaque: Wyndham Hall.

The house was old, not overly large, but it gave the impression of size and endurance, rather like its owner, Abigail Wentworth Wyndham. Somewhere between sixty and a hundred and sixty, Mrs. Wyndham was stout and energetic, and had been more than happy to rent one of her cottages to a friend of Joe's.

Okay, so Liz had lied a little. It was all for a good cause, right?

Fifty feet in, the gravel driveway split. The left branch snaked around to the rear of three of the six cottages; the right headed straight to the back of the other three. Each was swathed in soothing pastels, hers the palest peach. The neighbors on the left and right, granddaughters of Mrs. Wyndham, were away at college. A woman named Natalia Porter lived in the pink cottage across the way, and Pete Petrovski, a Copper Lake police officer, lived in the blue one. That meant the middle, lightest lavender cottage, its porch facing Liz's, was Joe's.

If ever a man could handle lavender, it was him.

She parked next to the house and climbed four steps to the porch. Opening the door, she stopped just inside, getting a feel for the place. Unlike her condo in Dallas, it was amazingly quiet. No traffic on nearby streets, no people hustling along crowded sidewalks, no jets roaring overhead on their way to or from the airport. When the refrigerator cycled on, she startled, then expelled the breath she'd subconsciously held.

This was going to take some getting used to.

The place was mostly empty; a wicker sofa and coffee table that had come from Mrs. Wyndham's porch, an assortment of pans and dishes and a borrowed air bed made up with borrowed sheets were all that surrounded her. *Just till you get some stuff of your own,* the landlady had said with a pat on Liz's arm.

Liz had no clue how long she'd be staying, but whether it was a week or a month, she would be fine with what was in the cottage now. She preferred take-out over cooking; the couch was comfortable; the coffee table could double as a desk; and the twin-sized air bed was no worse than the motel beds she slept in as often as her own.

A shout from out front drew her back through the house to watch a tan blur streak wildly around the stretch of grass that separated the two rows of cottages. A larger yellow blur followed, panting happily, and the girl from the coffee shop watched, her expression somewhere between scolding and laughing. Behind her, a bicycle was parked in front of the pink cottage, and beyond, the front door stood open, with the screen door shoved back so far that it hadn't closed again. Escape of the puppies, Liz surmised as she opened her own screen door and went outside to the front steps.

Immediately the dogs came racing in her direction, the tan one sleek and wiry, the yellow one larger, fuzzy—a Lab mix having a very bad hair day. Their wannabe mistress, who she guessed was Natalia Porter, turned her way, too, and all hint of pleasure disappeared from the girl's face. She looked at Liz's car and at the open door behind her, then scowled. "What are you doing here?"

"I'm your new neighbor. Liz Dalton." Instead of offering her hand, she crouched to scratch the puppies. They were too exuberant by half to be indoor dogs. For a moment they lolled and grunted appreciatively, then something caught their attention and they were off again.

"Joe wasn't happy to see you. Does he know you've moved in here?"

"He'll find out soon enough."

"He's not going to like it."

Because she couldn't disagree, Liz shrugged, then leaned one hip against the stair railing and studied Natalia. She was older than first glance suggested, although with her bottom lip edged out, she still resembled a pouty adolescent. Joe had been sitting with her when Liz walked into the coffee shop; they lived next door to each other. Just friends? Or more?

Judging from Natalia's animosity, Liz would guess *very* good friends, or the girl wanted a whole lot more.

A little jealousy somewhere deep inside her prickled. Did Joe go for the big-eyed, underfed waif type? Because if so, he couldn't possibly appreciate anything about *her.* She was so far off *that* target that she might as well be another life form.

But Joe's love life was none of her business. She was here to find out what he knew about Josh. No doubt the hostility he'd displayed toward his brother was genuine; she just didn't know whether he'd told the truth about not seeing him. Families tended to stick together. Seven years with the marshals service, and she hadn't yet met the family willing to turn on their loved one, no matter what he'd done.

"Your puppies are cute."

Natalia watched the dogs collide, then tumble across the grass, legs tangled together, and almost smiled. "They're not mine. I found them."

"Finders keepers doesn't apply?"

"Mrs. Wyndham says no."

"What are you going to do with them?"

"Joe's gonna keep them. First he said no, but then he got

distracted and said okay." Natalia gave a tiny grimace of a smile and grudgingly added, "Thanks."

So Liz's appearance had been enough of a distraction to make Joe agree to take two dogs he didn't want. It wasn't a warm welcome; she never expected those.

But it was something.

Raven was late coming into the shop. Joe waited on a few after-work customers, hiding his impatience to leave. Usually when he got antsy, he went for a bike ride. A fast twenty-five miles could work it right out of him. This evening he didn't have that option, at least not until he went home and faced Natalia, her puppies and her questions about Liz Dalton.

He couldn't believe Liz had tracked him down. When he left Chicago, he'd cut off contact with pretty much everyone but his parents, and they'd moved away, too, soon after. A few aunts and uncles knew where he'd gone, but most of them wouldn't tell anyone, not even Josh. Especially not Josh.

Besides, he didn't want to think that Josh was important enough to Liz that she'd bothered to track him down.

There's no accounting for taste, his grandmother used to say.

A muffled thud from the storeroom indicated Raven's arrival. He walked into the room, stopping so suddenly he practically toppled over. If he didn't know she was the only other person with a key to the shop, he would have thought a stranger had wandered in.

Gone was the jet-black hair that looked like it came straight from an ink bottle, and in its place was a warm, natural-looking brown. He'd never seen Raven with a hair color even close to natural. All the excess holes—lip, nose, brow, ears—were empty, and her makeup actually flattered her instead of making her look like a walking corpse. Add a green shirt and faded jeans in place of her usual black, and she looked normal. He'd *never* seen her looking normal.

First Liz Dalton showing up, then Raven transforming into the girl next door… This couldn't be good.

"What?" she asked hostilely, snapping Joe out of his shock. Hostility he was used to.

"Nothing. I'm out of here. Call me if you need anything." He wheeled his bike into the alley. As he tightened the strap of the helmet and swung one leg over the bike frame, he wondered what was responsible for Raven's new look.

Love or, at least, lust.

Look at Liz. She hadn't changed her appearance for Josh, but she'd surely lowered her standards. Women like her just didn't get involved with men like him. She was too smart, classy, law-abiding. At least, she *had* been. Who knew what all those months with Josh had done to her?

Now that he was gone, why was she looking for him? To renew the relationship? To punish him? To reclaim something he'd taken of hers?

Joe regretted not asking.

His edginess still sharp, he rode onto Oglethorpe, then made a left onto Calhoun. Too soon, he braked to turn into the Wyndham gate and bumped along the gravel road until he reached his house. Natalia's lime-green bike was parked next door, but there was no sign of her or the dogs he'd agreed to take in the stupidity of his fog over seeing Liz. Maybe she'd changed her mind. Maybe she'd decided that trying to hide them from Miss Abigail was worth a shot…though he couldn't imagine anything escaping the old woman's attention.

He'd reached the top of the steps when a screen door thumped shut. He was accustomed to neighbors on either side, but this sound had come from the other side of the yard. It was only Tuesday, so neither granddaughter would be home from college, and the middle house had stood empty longer than he'd lived there.

The hair on the back of his neck prickled. He didn't want to look over his shoulder. He'd done too damn much of that in the first six months out of the hospital; a balloon popping had been enough to make him dive for cover. But once he'd come to Copper Lake, the uneasiness had faded. He'd felt safe here.

But if Liz could find him, so could the Mulroney brothers, the Chicago businessmen who'd proven once that they couldn't tell the difference between him and Josh. Maybe if they did come around, he'd have time to show them the scars left from their previous run-in as proof. If they didn't kill him first and look later.

Slowly he turned. And stared.

Oh, man, hadn't he thought on seeing Raven that life was taking a turn for the worse?

Liz was seating herself on the top step of the cottage directly across the lawn. She'd changed into really short denim cutoffs that made her mile-long legs look two miles long, and topped them with a plain white T-shirt like those that filled his top dresser drawer. His had never looked that good.

Her olive skin damn near glowed in the late-afternoon sun, and her hair gleamed blue-black. *She's Italian,* Josh had said with a wink and a leer. *You know what that means. Hot-blooded as hell.*

Just looking at her made Joe's blood hot.

He should go inside his house. Lock the door. Pull the shades. Do his best, damn it, to pretend that he hadn't seen her again, that she wasn't sitting fifty feet away, that she'd never been Josh's girl.

Instead he slowly walked down the steps and across the yard. The grass was thick and smelled sweetly of spring and the promise of summer. He stopped ten feet from the porch and watched as Liz took a drink of bottled water.

Big mistake. He shouldn't be watching anything involving a mouth as sexy as hers. The plumping of her plum-colored lips as they closed around the bottle neck, the movement of muscles as the cold water flowed down her throat, the slight grip of pink-tipped fingers around the bottle's sweaty plastic…

Finally—thank God—she lowered the bottle and met his gaze. "Hello, neighbor."

He swallowed hard, his own mouth suddenly dry. "Do you know how many millions of those bottles wind up in landfills and how long they take to decompose? The least you could do is buy a gallon jug and drink it from a glass. Better yet, buy a filtering system, or hey, here's an idea—drink from the tap. It won't kill you."

She blinked, then looked at the bottle. "Sorry my drinking habits offend you."

Heat flushed through him. He wasn't a crusader. He did what he could to be environmentally responsible, but he didn't push it on others. But instead of apologizing, he asked, "Why are you here?"

"I told you. I'm looking for Josh."

"And I told you, I haven't seen or heard from him."

Her smile was small and tight. She didn't believe him. She thought he was protecting his seven-minutes-older brother. That just proved how little she knew him.

Of course, they didn't know each other at all. He'd seen her four times before the Mulroneys had tried to kill him in Josh's place. Four excruciating evenings with Josh between them.

Except that last time. For a few short minutes they'd been alone in the room, and the tension between them had been unbearable. They had almost touched that night—had almost kissed. But she had whispered exactly the right words to stop him, and he'd bolted from the room before his brother had returned.

Remember Josh.

That was probably the only time in his life he'd managed to forget him.

"So what do you think? That if you hang around here long enough, Josh will show up and prove me a liar?" He folded his arms over his chest. "You've mistaken me for my brother. I don't lie."

"Never?" she asked, one brow arched.

He'd fled the kitchen that night, nearly plowing over Josh on the way. *What's wrong?* he'd asked, and Joe had brushed him off. *Nothing. Everything's fine.* Except that he'd almost kissed his brother's girl. Except that he'd wanted a hell of a lot more than a kiss from her.

Now he just wanted her to go away.

"How did you get Miss Abigail to rent to you?" The old lady didn't need the income from the cottages. She only rented to people she knew and liked. She'd been a regular at the coffee shop for three months before she'd agreed to let him have the purple house.

"I told her you and I were old friends."

He scowled. "And she believed you?"

"And provided me with keys, furniture and dishes."

"I'll have to tell her you lied."

Liz's eyes widened innocently. "What kind of gentleman would do that?" Then she smiled. "See? I haven't mistaken you for your brother. No one would ever call Josh a gentleman."

It was an incredible smile, and it did incredible things to him. The knots in his gut changed to an entirely different kind of knot. Not stress, not anxiety, but tension of a much more intimate nature. He liked that smile. He could grow used to it very quickly. He could learn to need it.

If only he could also learn to forget.

Resolutely he stiffened his spine and scowled at her again. "Why are you looking for Josh?"

She took another drink from the bottle, her gaze on him as if expecting another lecture. After capping it, she set it aside, then rested her arms on her bent knees. "Let's just say he's got something I want."

It figured. His brother was a liar, a cheat, self-centered to the max and, now, a thief, too. "You won't find him hanging around me."

"Maybe not. But it's the last place I have to hang around."

"Leave your number and go back to Chicago. I'll call you if I hear from him."

She shrugged. "I'm in no hurry to get back. I'll stick around and experience Georgia in the springtime. Mrs. Wyndham says it's very nice."

He didn't say anything. He couldn't think of anything *to* say.

Pivoting on his heel, he stalked back across the grass to his own house. Before he reached it, though, Natalia's screen door slammed open and eight scrabbling feet dragged her onto the porch. He wasn't sure whether the yelps came from her or the lunging, yipping dogs she held, more or less, at the ends of two leashes. She scrambled down the steps, barely keeping both her balance and her hold on the leashes, then managed to dig in her heels as both dogs began sniffing and dancing around his feet.

Her smile was brave if not particularly confident as she offered the leashes to him. "Your puppies," she said breathlessly. "You'll love them."

He looked down at the dogs, one sniffing so fast that he was surprised it didn't hyperventilate and the other trying to climb up him with paws the size of salad plates. "Puppies," he repeated. He'd expected something small, cute and cuddly that would fall asleep with nothing more than a brief belly scratch. These two were both quivering nose to tail as if they might never sleep.

Liz, Raven and now this. Life was going downhill fast.

Chapter 2

Liz woke up at five-thirty without the help of an alarm, but her eyes were heavy and her brain slow to kick in as she crawled out of bed. After a stop in the bathroom, she padded into the living room to look across the grass at the lavender house. The windows were dark, and there was no sign of the black heavy-duty bike that was Joe's only mode of transportation.

Even back in Chicago, he'd been into recycling. Ever juvenile, Josh had thought it a hoot to toss out pop cans and newspapers when his brother was around. But she hadn't realized until prepping to come here that his commitment to going green extended to not even owning a car.

She felt a twinge of guilt when she opened the refrigerator and took out a bottled water and the foam container that held leftovers from last night's dinner.

She knew from her briefing that A Cuppa Joe opened at 6:00 a.m. Business was good enough that Joe had a part-time

helper, a retired schoolteacher by the name of Esther, from
opening until nine. There was another part-timer, Raven, who
worked from 5:00 p.m. until close. After Esther and before
Raven, Joe was usually on his own.

For at least part of that time today, he would have company.

She ate bites of cold vegetable lo mein while getting
dressed. Makeup done, hair pulled into a froth of curls on top
of her head, earrings matched to her cobalt-blue sheath, Liz
stepped into strappy sandals with three-inch heels, grabbed
her purse and went to her rental car.

The sky was turning rosy in the east, and lights were on in
most of the houses she passed on her way downtown. Back
home in Dallas, lights were always on, and morning traffic
was a nightmare. Chicago, where she'd spent two months
before the botched murder attempt sent her, Josh and the rest
of the team out of state, was the same. Copper Lake's early
morning traffic consisted of only an occasional car.

She parked in the same spot she'd taken the day before and
just sat for a moment. Most of the buildings that faced the
square were dimly lit, but A Cuppa Joe, Krispy Kreme and
Ellie's Deli were bright and welcoming. Visible through the
large window of the coffee shop, Esther, her hair a startling
orange, was filling mugs for seated customers while Joe was
behind the counter, a line of about ten waiting.

He moved quickly, efficiently, with a few words and an easy
smile for each customer. Two years ago, he'd been a destined-
for-success financial planner in one of Chicago's top investment
firms and had looked the part in Armani suits and Alden shoes.

He looked just as handsome and even a little sexier in
faded jeans and a pale blue T-shirt bearing the shop's logo.

She waited five, ten, twenty minutes, but business didn't
slack off. Finally she went inside, took a place at the end of the
line and waited, nerves tightening each time she moved forward.

Joe turned from the cash register and his smile disappeared. Mouth tightening at one corner, he curtly asked, "What do you want?"

She would bet this month's salary that his question had nothing to do with taking an order, but she smiled and gave one anyway. "Just plain coffee."

"Topéca, Jamaica Blue Mountain, Sumatra Mandehling?"

"You choose." Her coffee generally came crystallized in a jar and was reconstituted with microwaved water. She wasn't picky.

"To go?" There was a hint of hopefulness in his voice, although his expression remained impassive.

She smiled again. "No. I'll drink it here."

He bypassed the paper cups and cardboard sleeves, both bearing the emblem signifying recycled materials, and took a white ceramic mug from a shelf above the back counter. Dozens of mugs were lined up there, in all colors, sizes and designs, most marked with a regular's name. Natalia's was tall, pale yellow with emerald grass and a cartoon drawing of a lime-green bike.

Liz bet she could come in five times a day for a month and still not get her own mug added to the collection.

She paid no attention to the type of coffee he poured into the cup. It was steaming, fragrant and loaded with caffeine. That was all she needed. He traded the mug for the two bucks she offered without coming close to touching her, and he laid the change on the counter rather than in her outstretched hand.

Maybe some bit of sizzle remained on his part, after all.

She chose a table where her back was to the wall, not out of any sense of security but because it allowed her to see everyone in the shop and afforded a good view through the plate glass windows that lined the two outside walls.

Copper Lake had twenty thousand people or so and was prosperous for a small Southern town. The downtown was well-maintained and occupation of the buildings seemed about a hundred percent. The grass in the square was manicured, the flowerbeds were colorful and weed-free, and the gazebo bore a new coat of white paint. It looked like the small town of fiction: homey, welcoming, safe—a place where people looked out for each other.

Was that what had drawn Joe? Had he needed that sense of refuge?

She'd doctored her coffee with sweetener from a glass bowl in the middle of the table, stirred it with a real spoon and nursed her way through half of it when a presence disturbed the air. Glancing up, she met Joe's gaze, unsmiling, serious blue. At the moment, he looked as if the only thing he needed refuge from was her. She might feel something about that later. Regret. Disappointment. Maybe even satisfaction, that he felt enough of *something* to need to keep her at a distance.

He slid into the seat across from her, resting his hands on the table top. Good hands. Strong, tanned, long fingers, neat nails. "You were keeping Josh on a pretty short leash. How did he get away?"

She resented the idea that she was the clingy sort but could see why he thought so. From the time she'd been assigned to Josh's case, she'd rarely left his side.

Until the day he'd knocked her partner unconscious, handcuffed her to the bed and waltzed out of the San Francisco safe house where they'd been staying. She'd cursed herself hoarse and sworn that she would find him. Getting handcuffed, and to a bed, no less, by her protectee was the lowlight of her career.

"Everyone has to sleep sometime," she said with a shrug. She *had* been asleep when Josh had snapped the cuff on. Her partner, on the other hand, had merely been asleep on the job.

"Did you have a fight? Was he seeing someone else?"

She shrugged again, lazily, as if it didn't matter. "I'd say he just got tired of me." Being in protective custody wasn't easy for the most compliant of witnesses, and Josh had been far from that. He hadn't wanted to testify against the Mulroneys, but it was the only way to keep his own petty-criminal butt out of jail.

For an instant disbelief flitted across Joe's expression, but it was gone as quickly as she identified it. "What makes you think he'd leave Chicago? He's lived his whole life there. He likes it there."

She didn't just think Josh had left Chicago. She knew it. She sipped her coffee, lukewarm now, before pointing out, "You'd lived your whole life there, but you left."

Again, something flickered across his face. Guilt? Chagrin? Did he feel as if he'd run away? Getting the hell out of town when someone had tried to kill you, even if it was a case of mistaken identity, seemed perfectly rational to her. Instead of responding to her comment, though, he steered back to the original conversation. "When did he take off?"

"Two months ago."

"And you've been looking for him ever since."

She ignored the censure in his voice. There was something pathetic about a woman relentlessly tracking down the boyfriend who didn't want her anymore. But she'd given more than two years of her life to this case, and damned if Josh was going to blow it. He *would* testify even if she had to force him into court at gunpoint.

"It must be valuable."

"What?" she asked reflexively, drawing her attention back to Joe.

"Whatever he took."

Her smile felt thin and strained. "It is to me." Before he could continue with the questions, she asked one of her own. "Why Copper Lake?"

This time the shrug was his, a sinuous shifting of muscle beneath soft cotton. "The coffee shop was for sale. The price was right, the town was nice, and the name fit."

Her brows raised. "You didn't name it A Cuppa Joe?"

His scowl gave him a boyish look. "Do I look like the type who'd go for a name like that? I'd've chosen something less cute, like, I don't know, Not the Same Old Grind."

"I like A Cuppa Joe," she said stubbornly.

A raspy voice chimed in, "You and every single woman in town." Esther laughed, then topped off Liz's cup. "Are you single?"

"I am. Are you?"

"I am, too. I'd go after him, but that age thing is a problem. He's just way too old for my taste." Punctuating the words with a sly wink, Esther moved on with the pot to the next table.

Silence fell over the table, not uncomfortable but not comfortable either. Liz stirred sweetener into her refilled cup, the spoon clanking against the porcelain, casting about for something to say. The sight of an elderly man coming through the door with the assistance of a younger man, clearly his son, provided it. "How are your parents?"

"Considering that they had to leave the home they'd lived in for thirty-some years and move someplace where they knew no one, and they haven't seen their son in more than two years, not bad."

Once the Mulroneys had learned of Josh's family's existence—had found other targets for their warnings—the U.S. Attorney's office had deemed it safer for Joe and his parents to leave town and keep a low profile in their new homes. Joe had chosen the security of small-town life, while the elder Saldanas had opted for the anonymity of the city a short distance away. They'd been willing to give up a lot, but not the conveniences they'd taken for granted all their lives.

She had no desire to defend Josh's actions, but it seemed the sort of thing a girlfriend should do. "He didn't know how to contact them."

Not surprisingly, the argument didn't sit well with Joe. His gaze darkened and his lips thinned. "If he hadn't screwed up so damn bad, they would have stayed in that house forever, like they'd planned, and he'd have always known where to find them."

"He was sorry about that." Truthfully, in a few moments of remorse, Josh had expressed regret for what he'd put his family through. Those moments had been rare, though. More often, he'd blamed the Mulroneys, the marshals service and/or the U.S. Attorney's office. Sometimes he'd insisted that his parents had merely used Joe's shooting as an excuse to move to a warmer climate, a smaller city, a more retirement-friendly area—not that they'd ever expressed any dissatisfaction with Chicago.

Maybe, Liz had thought, he just couldn't face responsibility for the upheaval he'd caused.

Or he was just a self-centered, whiny brat.

Joe gave a sharp laugh. What it lacked in humor, it more than made up for with bitterness. "He's never been sorry for a damn thing in his life."

"He was sorry when you got shot. I saw him." That had been one of the rare occasions. Standing beside Joe's bed in ICU, not knowing whether he would survive, Josh had been humbled by regret and fear.

Liz had been afraid, too. Afraid that one more good guy would be lost, that once more the bad guys would win. Afraid that the Saldanas would never recover from such a loss. Afraid that she would always wonder what might have been if things had been different.

She had wondered. Nearly two years in different cities and states had added up to a lot of solitary nights. It had been safe to wonder then, because she'd thought she would never see Joe again. Once the Mulroneys went to trial and Josh had testified, she would take on new cases in new places. She would meet other men and probably, eventually, hopefully, fall in love with one of them.

Instead, here she was, sitting across from Joe, trying really hard not to wonder anymore.

She expected another denial from him, but it didn't come. He stared out the window for a moment, as if the increasing traffic held his interest, before finally dragging his gaze back to her. "Did he know? Did he know they wanted him dead?" he pressed on. "Did he let me go on with life as usual knowing that people wanted to kill him, that they could easily mistake me for him?"

Her fingers tightened around the mug. Were these the first questions he would ask his brother if given the chance? Would a *no* provide any comfort? Would *yes* destroy their relationship for all time?

Up to the day Joe was shot, the Mulroneys' crimes had been nonviolent. Their business had been just that: a routine job moving a product—money—from one place to another, laundering it along the way. They'd been involved in their communities; they'd gone to church with their families; they'd handled disputes diplomatically. Their hit on Josh had been the first and, so far, only sign of violence in their fifteen-year career. It was even possible that someone else Josh had pissed off was behind it instead.

"You know Josh." Liz's shrug was awkward. She'd never gotten over the guilt because *she* had known Josh, too. She should have expected violence. She should have known Joe was in danger. She should have protected him, too. "Nothing he ever does has consequences."

Yeah, Joe thought grimly. He knew Josh. "When we were

five, he sneaked Mom's keys out and took the car for a drive. He made it two blocks before he ran into two other cars. He wasn't hurt, but it did a lot of damage to all three vehicles. Mom spanked him. Dad grounded him, gave him extra chores, took his allowance, and three weeks later, Mom caught him behind the wheel again with the keys in the ignition. When we were eight, he tried to fly from our tree house to the ground. He spent the next six weeks with his left arm in a cast, spanked, grounded, extra chores, the whole bit again, and the day the cast came off, he tried again, breaking his right arm. And when we were twelve…" Breaking off, he shook his head. Too bad he couldn't banish the memory so easily.

"And you were always the good son."

He raised one hand in the Boy Scout saluté. "I made good grades, stayed out of trouble and never gave Mom and Dad a reason to worry."

"I was the good child, too," Liz said.

The simple statement stuck him as odd. He'd seen her as only two things: his brother's girlfriend and therefore the last woman on earth he should be—but was—attracted to. He'd never thought of her as a person: a daughter, a sister, someone with a life, hopes and plans outside of Josh.

Hell, he'd tried his best not to think of her at all.

"Of course, it wasn't difficult. I was the youngest of four and the only girl, so my parents were predisposed to think of me as the good kid whether I was or not."

Where were those brothers when she'd gotten involved with Josh? While Josh liked a challenge, he also liked not getting his ass kicked for messing around with the wrong girl. He would have kissed her goodbye…and then Joe, with his regular job, arrest-free record and all-around good-guy-ness, might have had a chance.

"Did your brothers approve of Josh?"

"They didn't meet him, but no, they wouldn't have approved."

Which had probably been part of Josh's appeal. Always being the good girl had grown tedious, and what better way for a good girl to rebel than with a bad boy?

Had she had enough of him now? Was she willing to admit he was a lost cause?

She was in Georgia looking for him after he'd dumped her and run. That seemed a pretty loud *No*.

"Do they live in Chicago?"

She picked up the mug, glanced at the dregs inside, then set it down again before meeting his gaze. Joe had the clear blue eyes that people paid money to get with contact lenses, but he'd always been a sucker for brown eyes, especially big, deep brown ones that, even after a couple of tough years, still managed a hint of innocence.

"No. D.C., Miami, L.A." After another pause, she added, "I guess we all wanted out of Kansas."

A good girl looking to escape the Kansas farmland and run a little wild. How easy it must have been for Josh to wrap her around his finger.

"I never would have pegged you for a farm girl."

She blinked, then laughed, an easy, natural sound that reminded him again of innocence. "I've never set foot on a farm in my life. Well, no, wait, there was the time in third grade that my parents took us to the pumpkin patch for Halloween. That *might* have been a farm. Then again, it might have been a church parking lot in Wichita." Her voice turned chiding. "There's more to Kansas than farms."

"I'll keep that in mind in case I ever head out there. Do you go back often?"

"At least twice a year to see my parents." As Esther approached with the coffee carafe again, Liz shook her head with a faint smile. "Do you get to see much of your parents?"

He shrugged. They'd settled in Savannah, only a few hours away, and he drove down at least once a month. He didn't tell her that, though. How could he be sure that Josh hadn't sent her here with a made-up story about looking for him just so he could find their folks? Mom and Dad might miss him like hell, but they were better off without him. Who knew what kind of trouble Josh would bring to their door if he could find it?

Because his thoughts had already taken a grim turn, he remarked, "Miss Abigail says you signed a month's lease." Twenty-nine more nights like last night, his gaze straying constantly to the windows, watching shadows as she moved from room to room. Twenty-nine more nights of getting to know her schedule, of catching unexpected glimpses of her, of seeing her both at home in casual clothes—those snug denim cutoffs from last night still made him sweat—and out and dressed up.

Twenty-nine more nights. God help him.

"Actually, my lease is for one month, with a month-by-month extension. I could be here one, two, four months. As long as it takes." She made the announcement with an entirely too-sunny attitude. It turned his mouth down as if he'd just taken a hearty swallow of the used-up coffee grounds he provided Miss Abigail for her garden.

"If you're really looking for Josh, Copper Lake isn't the place to do it."

"It's the only place I have." The airiness disappeared and something else crossed her face, flattening her voice. Panic? Despair? He'd taken something of value from her, she'd said. Sentimental value, like her grandmother's opal ring she'd once worn? It was missing from her finger now.

Or financial value? Liz must have worked during the months they were together; someone had to support them, preferably in a way that didn't bring them to the attention of the local cops.

Had Josh wiped out her savings before he ran? Joe didn't know what kind of work she did—Josh's tastes usually ran toward waitresses—but it didn't seem likely she could have saved an amount substantial enough to make her track him down.

What else could make a reasonably intelligent woman chase after a man she was well rid of? Love, he supposed, though he'd rather not think of Liz in love with his brother.

A knock on the plate glass window drew his gaze outside, and he waved. Anamaria Calloway, dressed in red with a bright Caribbean print shawl wrapped around her shoulders, was pushing the stroller that held young Will. The baby was sucking a pacifier and surveying the world around him with a lazy certainty that he was the center of its existence. He got both laziness and certainty, along with blue eyes, from his daddy and everything else, they hoped, from his ma—

He jerked his gaze back to Liz. "You aren't— You didn't—"

She looked from him to the baby, then back to him with nothing less than horror on her face. "Have a baby? With Josh? Dear God, no."

Joe didn't want to examine just how relieved he was by the answer. Knowing Josh had a kid would be tough enough. Knowing that he had a kid with Liz... Of all the things his brother had done in the last thirty years, that one would be the deal breaker. No more contact. Ever.

"I would never be so careless," Liz said, her tone gone from shock to huffiness.

"People forget. They have accidents."

"Not me. Never."

"You never get so carried away that you don't remember, or you don't think it'll be all right just this one time?"

"Never."

Joe wasn't smiling because he liked the emphatic nature of

her answer. It wasn't really a smile at all. He was just letting some of the tension ease from his muscles. "Do you ever wonder if maybe you've been sleeping with the wrong guys?"

Again, she blinked, but this time there was no tinkling laugh to follow it. "I think we got off track."

"From the day we met," he muttered. He couldn't tell whether she'd heard. Her cheeks were flushed and she was looking just a bit disconcerted. Good. Making her lose her emotional balance might help him keep his.

"We were talking about the odds of my finding Josh here."

"We hadn't gotten to odds yet, but I'd guess they're about a million to one against you. You familiar with the phrase 'gone to ground'? Because Josh is. He's had regular hideouts since he was three, and 'with me' has never been one of them, so you might as well move on."

"You haven't seen him."

"Not since the day I got shot."

"You haven't talked to him."

He shook his head.

"No e-mail. No contact with him at all."

He held her gaze but didn't speak. If she took his silence for a negative, if he'd deliberately misled her, well, that *Thou shalt not lie stuff* was between him and God. Certainly not him and Josh's ex-maybe-wannabe-again-girlfriend. Besides, an unsolicited envelope in the mail with no return address didn't count.

"See those two guys over there?" He gestured to the table closest to the door. "That's Detective Tommy Maricci and Lieutenant A. J. Decker of the Copper Lake Police Department. If Josh showed up here, they'd be the first people I'd call. And he knows that. I'm fresh out of excuses, sympathy and family ties. He'd have to be beyond desperate to come to me because I'm not risking my ass for him ever again. So…" He shoved his chair back with a scrape. "You're wasting your time hanging out here."

"Well, it's my time to be wasted, isn't it?"

He couldn't argue that point with her, so instead he picked up her cup and spoon and headed for the counter.

It was her time, Liz reflected as she stood up. And though she was there for the job, it left her an awful lot of nothing to do. Watching Joe chat with the two police officers he'd pointed out, she strolled across the café, then outside. The morning air was cool and damp and tinged with the promise of later heat. She could walk around the square and familiarize herself with the area. She could meet Joe's business neighbors and see what they had to say about him. Most people, she'd found, told strangers way too much about others. Usually there was no malicious intent; they just forgot that they couldn't trust strangers anymore.

How long had it been since she'd been so naive? She'd had a wonderful upbringing; there was no doubt about that. She'd loved her parents and her brothers, and they'd loved her. But discussions at the family dinner table had revolved around law and order, crime and punishment. She'd thought all little girls' daddies wore suits, guns and badges to work; that all little girls' mommies put bad people in prison; that all kids, even the good ones, borrowed Dad's handcuffs for show-and-tell at least once and chained the prissiest girl in class to the teacher's desk.

Your family's weird, her best friend had told her in third grade, and Liz had put her in a wrist lock, forced her to her knees and made her apologize.

It had taken some time for her to realize they *were* different. With a grandfather and a father who were deputy U.S. Marshals, two uncles with the FBI, an aunt in the DEA and a mother who was a criminal court judge, they hadn't been the typical Midwest family. Her grandfather was retired, and her father was close to it, but now her brothers were working with NCIS, ATF and the U.S. Attorney General's office.

She walked to the end of the block, passing neatly kept storefronts, a flower shop that smelled heavenly through the open door and Ellie's Deli, with enticing scents drifting through her open door, too. The cold lo mein she'd had for breakfast seemed a long time ago, so Liz climbed the old-fashioned porch and stepped inside.

The place was charming: old to its very bones, with fresh paint and reproduction fabrics and a few good antiques. Even though a fair number of tables were occupied, the bulk of the deli's morning rush centered on the takeout counter, a wavy-glassed cabinet that looked as if it might have displayed pies and pastries once upon a time.

"Table or takeout?" a waitress asked on her way to the kitchen with an armload of plates.

"Table, please." *Right in the middle of the gossips, if you don't mind.*

Instead of leading her toward the dozen old men sharing a country-fried breakfast and their opinions on everything, the waitress turned toward the back of the building. The broad hall opened into a smaller, quieter dining room. Only two tables were occupied there: one by the pretty black woman with the baby stroller and a man Liz assumed, by their matching gold bands, was her husband and the one person in town, after Joe, who most interested Liz.

Natalia Porter's attention was riveted outside, where the two puppies, restrained by leashes attached to the fence, were digging furiously in the dirt. The tan one created a hole deep enough to plunge her entire head into it, withdrawing only to snap at the fuzzy one when he tried to join her. Chastened, he went back to his own digging, shifting position just enough that the dirt his paws sent flying landed on the sleek puppy's back.

Natalia laughed out loud before abruptly realizing that Liz was standing at the next table. For an instant, sullenness crossed her face, then her expression went blank.

"They're adorable," Liz remarked. She pulled a chair from the table so both Natalia and the puppies were in easy view. "Do they have names yet?"

"No. Joe has to name them."

"So they're well and truly his."

Surprise darkened the girl's eyes—today, sapphire blue at the outer rims, radiating in to pale gray—then she nodded. "Naming things helps form attachments."

Natalia certainly had an attraction to Joe, even though he'd obviously not been part of her naming. Liz would like to know what that attachment was, how deep it ran and whether it was one-sided.

For business reasons, of course. Everything she knew about a subject added to her investigation. She wasn't allowed to have a personal interest. That had never been a problem for her before. But now...

The waitress came for her order. After glancing at Natalia's plate—ham, biscuits and gravy, hash browns with cheese, and hotcakes—and her stick-slender body, then thinking about her own curves that could so easily become dangerous, Liz asked for a fruit plate and unsweetened tea. Natalia remained silent, looking away from the dogs only to take a bite of food.

After Liz's fruit arrived, she asked the girl, "Been a long time since you've had pets of your own?"

Natalia glanced at her. "I never have had," she said flatly, then looked off as if she'd given away too much about herself.

Instead of questioning her, Liz speared a piece of pineapple on her fork. "I grew up with three brothers. We always had dogs, cats, turtles, fish, spiders and snakes. The snakes were for my benefit. My brothers liked to sneak them into my bed when I was asleep. One morning I woke up with one of the snakes looking me in the eye, smiling this damn smile while it flicked its tongue at me. Once my terror receded, I put it in a box, waited until that night when Mom's boss came over for dinner and set it loose on the table. He was freaked out, his wife and daughters were in hysterics, and the next day all the snakes were out of the house for good."

Natalia shuddered. "I hate snakes."

"Me, too. But I couldn't let my brothers know how much they scared me, or they would have won. You know?"

Slowly Natalia nodded and something in her expression said she really did know. She'd faced something that scared her, had hidden her fear and stood up to it, because she'd needed to win.

Liz couldn't help but wonder what; it was her nature to want answers. An abusive father? A violent boyfriend? A threatening boss?

It would take more time than either of them had for Liz to gain her trust and find out. Instinct told her that Natalia Porter was a woman, despite her waifish look, who had little truth to tell and less trust to give.

"Have you always lived here?" she asked before sliding a piece of sweet melon into her mouth.

Natalia's expression was torn, as if she'd rather pretend Liz wasn't there but had already figured out that wasn't the way to get rid of a nosy person. "No. Just a few months."

"Where did you come from?"

Her only answer was a shrug.

"What made you choose Copper Lake?"

"Luck of the draw. The road went left, right and straight. I went straight, and it brought me here."

"There are worse ways to decide where you're going to

stay awhile." Like providing security to someone who couldn't make up his mind whether he wanted or needed it. Liz had worked protective custody before, but never with someone as difficult as Josh.

"I don't have to ask why you're here, do I?" Natalia pushed her plate away, the luscious cheese-covered hash browns untouched, and shifted in her chair to face Liz. "Because of Joe. Are you and he…?"

Liz signaled the waitress for a refill. "We know each other."

"Duh. Like that wasn't obvious yesterday. How well?"

Not well enough. Thanks to Josh, they would probably never get to know each other well enough. Either the older Saldana twin would be dragged out of the hole he'd hidden in and would testify against the Mulroneys, or the trial would come and go without his input. Either way, Liz would go on to a new case, and Joe would go on with his new life, and she, for one, would have a whole lot of regrets.

"I used to date Joe's brother," Liz said evenly.

The relief that flashed through Natalia's eyes was intense, there and gone, and generated a similar intensity in Liz's gut. The look that replaced it was flatter, blanker than usual.

Like those adoring teenagers in the coffee shop yesterday, Natalia had a thing for Joe. The big question was what he felt for her. Was it mutual, or was she hanging around waiting for him to finally notice that she was a very pretty woman with porcelain skin, delicate bones, eyes big enough to drown in and a perfect Cupid's bow to shape her lips?

Liz would like to believe Joe was as oblivious to Natalia's crush as he'd been to the teenagers', but that would be naive, and she tried to never be naive. Joe and Natalia were friends; they lived next door to each other. She was enough of a regular at his shop to merit her own mug. He'd noticed she was beautiful.

Saldana men always noticed beauty, Josh had often bragged.

"So…are you and Joe…?" Liz hoped for the same sort of dear-God-no reaction she'd had to Joe's suggestion that she'd gotten pregnant by Josh.

Natalia showed no emotion at all. "Would it matter to you if we are?"

Like hell, and that was a problem. Federal agents did not get romantically involved with any subject in an investigation—not suspects, not witnesses, not victims, not other agents. Not, not, *not.*

How did you stay uninvolved when you'd lost control? When your brain and logic and reason and ethics screaming *no* couldn't be heard over the pounding of your heart?

The first thing you did was lie. To others. To yourself.

"Joe's life is none of my business. I'm just looking for Josh."

Natalia's Cupid's-bow mouth took on a pinched look. She didn't believe Liz.

Which was only fair, because Liz didn't believe herself.

Chapter 3

Joe's primary function at any of the various organizational meetings he attended was to provide the coffee. Oh, he knew Ellie Maricci and the others relied on his willingness to volunteer, but when all was said and done, it was the coffee that counted most.

Tonight's meeting was at River's Edge, the antebellum beauty catty-cornered from A Cuppa Joe. It was a tourist attraction, a community meeting center and *the* place for celebrations of every sort. His mother, Dory, had seen a story about it in the Savannah newspaper and commented—while gazing at Joe with utter innocence—what a lovely place it would be for a wedding. *The ceremony in the garden, a string quartet on the verandah, a lavish cake in the gazebo and laughter everywhere.* The wistfulness in her voice had been deep, tinged with sadness.

Like most mothers, Dory wanted grandbabies to cuddle,

preferably after a wedding to remember, but, she was fond of saying, she would take them any way she could get them. A bride who needed a little help planning a wedding would have been a plus in her book. She understood it was the bride's mother who traditionally got the pleasure, but didn't she deserve something extra for raising him and Josh?

She'd deserved a lot better than she'd gotten.

All too aware of that, Joe had responded with a joke. *How do you get decent blues out of a string quartet?*

Predictably, she'd swatted him. *You don't play the blues at a wedding.*

Depends on whose wedding, his father, Ruben, had muttered.

Blues would be most appropriate for the poor sucker who made the mistake of walking down the aisle with Josh. Better yet, a funeral dirge.

And it damn well had better not be Liz.

Scowling, Joe carried a wicker basket across the verandah and through the open double doors. Ellie had covered half of the antique cherrywood dining table with desserts from the deli's kitchen and left the other half for him. He'd already delivered two urns, started the coffee brewing—Guatemalan Antiqua and Ethiopian Yirgacheffe—and from the basket he now unloaded bowls of sugar and sweetener and two small carafes of cream, one plain, one flavored with hazelnut.

"Oh, my gosh, it smells wonderful in here." Ellie waited for him to turn away from the table, then hugged him. Her body was solid, warm, with a barely noticeable bump from her four-months-along pregnancy. For more than five years, she and Tommy had gotten together, broken up and done it all over again, all because of his desire to get married and have kids and her opposition to both ideas.

Funny how surviving a near-death experience had made her see things in a different light.

It was one thing Joe and Ellie had in common. The near-death experience. Not so much the desire to marry and have kids.

When she stepped back, he gestured toward the table. "Do I need to set out cups and napkins again, or do you have that covered?"

Ellie grinned. "I brought finger food. No need for dishes."

"Yeah, well, I've seen people take their coffee directly from the urn, on their knees, scalding their tongues. It's not a pretty—"

The door that led from the dining room directly into the kitchen bumped open an inch or two, and black curls appeared briefly before the door received a harder shove. Liz was smiling, saying something over her shoulder and carrying a silver tray loaded with cups and saucers as she came into the room. Speaking of pretty sights…

Damn. He'd thought since he'd made it the rest of the day without so much as a glimpse of her that he might be safe. He would come to the meeting, it would be late when he got home, he would go straight to bed without even thinking about her…

Yeah, right.

"Hi, Joe."

He automatically reached for the tray, heavier than it should have been. She flashed him a smile, hotter than it should have been. "Thanks," she said as she began unloading cups and carefully lining them up near the urns. "I wondered why we were using the good china instead of paper plates and foam cups. Guess I have my answer."

We. How easily she included herself among his friends, his town. She'd been there less than thirty hours, already had an invitation to work on Ellie's project and had apparently made herself at home. Though, to be fair, Ellie would accept help from any living, breathing body.

And Liz was definitely living…breathing…and what a

body. She wore white capris that left her legs bare from the knee down, a black-and-white dotted shirt that clung to her curves and black-and-white dotted sandals. With heels, of course.

Had he mentioned that he liked sexy shoes?

Ellie began stacking the saucers around the dessert plates as she primly said, "I admire Joe's commitment to the environment and avoiding unnecessary waste."

"Of course you do, because it means when we do this type of thing, I do the dishes."

Liz wasn't fooled. "I saw the state-of-the-art dishwashers in there."

He shrugged.

"But tell me, doesn't it take a lot of energy to run the dishwasher, heat the water, dry the dishes—heavens, to manufacture and ship the dishwasher in the first place? How do you know it's not more environmentally friendly to just use throwaways and be done with it? Not foam, of course. It's practically indestructible. But paper decomposes."

Before he could respond, Ellie raised both hands. "Please, no environmental discussions. Tonight's for *my* cause."

Still holding Liz's gaze, Joe directed his words to Ellie. "I heard you'd decided to use environmentally friendly disposable diapers for the kiddo. And that your remodel includes solar panels and a geothermal heat pump system."

"That's our contractor's idea. Nothing to do with you," she replied with a wink for Liz's benefit. She knew Tommy and Russ had discussed it with him before making their choices. "So…I didn't realize you two had met."

"I didn't realize *you* two had met," he said.

Liz's movements were fluid as she took a cup from the table, placed it under the spout of the Antiqua urn and filled it. "A good cup of coffee is the first thing I look for in a new town," she said breezily.

"I'd've thought it would be a familiar face," Joe said without a hint of breeze.

Ellie's gaze shifted from one to the other, then she began easing away. "I'm gonna see if everyone's here. When you hear me talking loudly in the parlor, that's your cue to come on in. I'd hate for you to miss out on anything."

Liz stirred sugar into her coffee, then held the spoon to drip. "I think that means *she* doesn't want to miss out on anything."

"What are you doing here?"

"I met Ellie at the deli this morning. Cute names in this town. Ellie's Deli. A Cuppa Joe."

"Not my doing," he reminded her.

She nodded, then sucked the spoon into her mouth. The action was simple, unaffected, and damn near cut his knees out from under him. "Mmm. You know, there really is a difference between instant coffee and this stuff."

"Yeah." Was his voice really that hoarse? "Lucky for me, everyone else in the world was quicker than you to figure that out, or I'd be out of business."

She took a sip and made another, softer *mmm* sound. "I don't have time to make real coffee every day."

"You can't spare a few minutes? Keeping up with Josh— or tracking him down—must be a full-time job."

A blink, one blink of those java-dark eyes, was her only response to the mention of his brother, and he tried to read a lot into it. Did she love him? Did she miss him? Did she hate him, need him, want to punish him?

Did she see him every time she looked at Joe?

Being an identical twin had its pluses and minuses. Being hot for a woman who didn't even have to close her eyes to imagine she was with his brother was right up at the top of the minus column, along with being mistaken for him by a hitman.

Thinking about being hot for his brother's maybe-ex was

the perfect time for an interruption, provided by A. J. Decker. "Come on, Saldana. You've got all the coffee a man could need all day long. Do you mind sharing a little of it tonight?"

Joe forced his gaze from Liz. "I don't know. I'm so used to getting paid for it that it's kind of hard to give it away free."

Decker reached into his pocket and pulled out a wrinkled five. "Now will you move?"

Liz set her cup aside and picked up a clean one. "Keep your money, Lieutenant. This one's on me." Her slender, elegant fingers gestured toward the engraved plates that hung from each urn. "What's your pleasure?"

Pleasure? On her? Sweet hell, Joe had to get away. Fast. Saying, "Excuse me," and sounding more than a little strangled, he escaped the dining room for the broad hallway that divided the house front to back. The air was cooler there, easier to force into his choked lungs, kinder to his hot skin.

Familiar voices came from the parlor across the hall. Ellie and Tommy. The Calloway boys: Russ, Robbie and half-brother Mitch, and their wives, Jamie, Anamaria and Jessica. Sophy from the quilt shop and Officer Pete Petrovski, Joe's neighbor. KiKi Isaacs, the first female detective in Copper Lake history. Dharma, the temperamental chef at the deli, and Cate Calloway, ER doctor and former cousin by marriage to the Calloway boys. Marnie, the lost-in-another-world crime scene tech who oversaw the CLPD lab. Her people skills mostly applied to the recently dead, but Joe liked her anyway.

He liked all these people. He liked their parents and their kids and their dogs, and they liked him back, even if they didn't know much about him. The only person in town who did know much about him was approaching from behind, talking freely with Decker.

"...don't know how long I'll be here. I've just reached one of those points, you know, where anywhere you're not has

got to be better than where you are. If I like it, if I don't…"
She finished with a little shimmy of movement that started
with the wild curls gathered on top of her head and ended
with the slight sway of the ruffles stretched across the base
of her toes.

And Decker didn't even seem affected. His fingers didn't
tighten on the cup he held in his left hand. The saucer in his
right didn't tremble. He didn't look as if all the air had been
sucked out of his lungs with that one little wiggle. He just
nodded, said something about Dallas making Copper Lake
look damn good, shoved a bite of minicheesecake in his
mouth and went off to take a seat next to Cate.

Huh.

As Ellie moved to stand in front of the fireplace, Joe chose
the broad sill of a window to lean against. The windows were
open, and scents drifted in, along with the hum of insects and
the infrequent traffic on the street. He rested his hands on the
aged wood, settling in to relax and listen.

Ellie had already explained the gist of her plan to him: She
wanted to found a school for young women on the streets
who'd fallen through the system's cracks. Whether a girl ran
away or was tossed out by her parents, there was precious little
help available and virtually none after they turned eighteen.
Society got to wash their hands of them once the girls reached
the age of majority, leaving them on the streets with one job
skill—prostitution—and little more than dreams of having a
normal life.

Joe was all in favor of normal lives.

The location was the simplest of the problems. The Cal-
loways' mother, Sara, owned an abandoned elementary
school, and she was ready to donate it. But there were still the
legal issues, the zoning, the licensing, the funding, the staff.
But if anyone could handle it, he had faith these people could.

* * *

"It all sounds very daunting," Liz remarked two hours later when she delivered a tray of dirty dishes to the kitchen.

Joe glanced up from the sink where he was washing saucers. "Maybe to mere mortals."

"And these people aren't?"

"Oh, they're mortal enough. They're just…passionate."

Instead of murmuring some response, then leaving for more dishes, she picked up a dish cloth from the neat stack on the counter and began drying a fragile cup. "You included?"

"Only about my coffee."

"And your family."

He lifted one shoulder in agreement. "You know, passion can be positive or negative."

"Oh, I'm sure you use your power for good. Getting on board with this bunch. All the recycling stuff. Coaching Little League. Sponsoring needy families at Christmas. Taking in strays." She searched the cabinets until she found the remaining coffee cups, placed that one inside, then came back for another. "I've been talking to people about you."

He gave her a flat look. "They know what I want them to know."

"Uh-huh."

"No one knows what happened in Chicago or about Josh."

"Oops. I told Natalia that Josh and I used to date."

He washed a few more dishes before brushing it off. "Natalia doesn't make small talk."

"I noticed. Talking with her is like pulling teeth. I had breakfast next to her. I helped her walk those dogs back to your house. I even cleaned up the fuzzy one's accidents on the way, and she still didn't say three dozen words to me." She watched, wondering if he would defend Natalia, certain he wouldn't betray any of her confidences.

He didn't surprise her. "You're lucky it was the fuzzy one. His really are accidents. The brown one, though…she does everything on purpose."

"She's just a puppy," Liz said with a laugh.

"She's a half-starved, abandoned puppy who thinks she rules the world, particularly any corner of it that I try to claim for my own. She's clearly familiar with the phrase 'alpha,' but she doesn't seem to know that it's usually followed by 'male.' She tries to mount the male, she stands me down and she's not afraid to draw blood if you cross her."

"Wow, and you've only had her twenty-four hours. This should be fun."

With a scowl, he settled another stack of plates into the soapy water.

Liz became aware of the murmuring voices outside the kitchen growing more distant. "Sounds as if everyone's leaving."

"You thought I was kidding when I said I do dishes?"

"I thought surely someone would help."

"Someone is helping." He gestured to her with a sudsy hand. "Believe me, they pay attention. If you hadn't stayed, Sophy would have, or Ellie or Jamie. The moment they see a willing victim walk through the door, though, they're outta here."

A willing victim—that was her. And Josh. But not Joe. He hadn't asked for any part of the events that had turned his life upside down. Did he regret it? The shooting, of course. But moving to Copper Lake, starting his own business, making new friends?

"Do you regret it?" For an instant she was surprised that she'd asked the question aloud, but because she couldn't take back the words, she pushed on. "Moving. Starting over. Moving *here*."

He washed the last dish, then started on the glass urns. "It wasn't in my life plan."

"But sometimes good comes out of bad. You seem happier here than you were in Chicago."

"You should have seen me before yesterday," he said drily. "I was damn near ecstatic."

She made a face at his back, then turned her attention to the kitchen. It was lovely, looking every one of its two-hundred-plus years but with all the modern conveniences, including the two dishwashers she'd mentioned earlier. She wasn't surprised Joe had chosen not to use them. The dishes weren't heavily soiled and could be done just as quickly by hand. Even she probably would have gone that route.

After the paper plates and cups had been prohibited.

"So what's kept you busy the last two years? Besides Josh, of course. You never seemed to have time for work in Chicago."

Meaning he'd never seen her unless she was plastered hip-to-thigh to Josh. Except that one night. That was the closest she'd ever come to disaster, and that included waking up to find Josh handcuffing her to the bed *and* spending two years on the fugitive squad.

"I've done a lot of things. I usually work for a while, save some money, then take a break."

"What kind of things?"

"Wait tables. Tend bar. Clerical stuff." Josh had thought it funny to tell a few of his buddies that she worked out of their apartment as a phone-sex operator. Joe wouldn't be nearly as amused by that as those guys had been. *Talk dirty to me* had become their standard greeting to her.

"Most people who work those kinds of jobs have to keep working. They don't get the luxury of months off here or there."

She hadn't had an entire month off since college, and even then she'd worked part-time jobs. But she smiled sunnily and said, "Most people have obligations."

"And all you want to do is find Josh."

Ignoring his comment, she put away the last half dozen cups, laid the damp towels across a rod to dry and leaned against the countertop to watch him rinse the first urn. It was tall, the glass tempered, distorted to give the appearance of age. He didn't take particular care with it but handled it competently, the way he'd handled the more delicate cups and plates. She knew without asking that he'd never broken a piece of the everyday china, never let a soapy urn slip from his hands, never lost his cool, calm confidence.

Except maybe a little, on an emotional level. When it came to Josh. And her.

If he were anyone else, she would like that she could throw him off his emotional balance.

If she were anyone else, she would take a chance at letting him unbalance her.

He finished the last of the cleanup in silence, then scooped up the urns, one in each arm. "Can you flip the light switch?"

Accommodatingly she followed him through the house, turning off the switches he indicated, picking up the wicker basket from the dining table, securing the double doors behind them.

It was nearly ten o'clock. The buzz of streetlamps was louder than the tree frogs' song, but only by a notch or so. The scents of the river two blocks away mingled with the closer fragrance of flowers, and music drifted from somewhere nearby, something low and mournful.

Liz took a deep breath and let it out on a sigh. "You made a good choice." Sensing rather than seeing Joe's curious look, she went on. "Coming to Copper Lake. Do you ever remember a night this calm in Chicago?"

"Hundreds of them. It's just a town, too."

"A great big, sprawling, noisy, crowded town."

"Too big for the Kansas farm girl?"

She responded with an exaggerated frown before following him around the corner of the verandah, then down brick steps to the path. There she moved to walk beside him, through the gate and onto the sidewalk. "I'm not a farm girl."

Stopping beside her car, he shifted the urns, then extended his hand for the basket. She considered not giving it to him and instead heading across the street to the coffee shop, prolonging this moment with him. A short walk in the cool humid night, a few moments more of comfortable conversation, another few deep breaths that smelled of jasmine and coffee and faded cotton…

She gave him the basket. "I'll see you later."

His fingers brushed hers. "You'll be hard to avoid."

She shoved her hands into her pockets. "You know how to get rid of me for good." *Tell me where Josh is.*

There at the side of the street, his arms loaded, still looking like a surfer boy but a tired one, he said flatly, "I can't tell you what I don't know."

His voice lacked the insistence she was accustomed to from deceitful family members. He didn't shift his weight or avoid her gaze or do anything to suggest dishonesty. That didn't mean he was telling the truth, though. It just meant he was better at lying than most people she dealt with. He was smart enough to avoid the usual subconscious behaviors of an untruthful person.

"Like I said, I'll see you." She clicked the remote to unlock the car door, then slid behind the wheel. He didn't wait until she was safely on her way, but turned and strode across two intersections to the dimly lit coffee shop on the corner.

Within three minutes, she was home. In six, she was stretched out on the sofa, her cell phone propped to her ear. The only light burning in the house was above the kitchen sink; it cast just enough illumination to deepen the living room shadows. The curtains were drawn back, giving her a good view of all three houses across the way.

Pete Petrovski was home, and so was Natalia, babysitting Joe's puppies. Their barks drifted through the open window, along with a cooling breeze. But the lavender cottage remained dark. Liz wondered if Joe was still at the shop, or if he'd taken advantage of the lovely night to take a ride around town, or if he'd somehow managed to sneak in through the back so he wouldn't risk seeing her. Not an easy feat considering none of the houses had back doors.

"Hey, I know you've had a tough day playing the grasping ex-girlfriend, but surely it wasn't so exhausting that you can't take part in a conversation for five minutes." Mika Tupolev's voice was chiding, but her expression, Liz knew from experience, wouldn't match. Mika didn't frown or scowl or sneer or smirk, or smile much, for that matter. Like the icy Russian mountains her family had once called home, she was all cool all the time. The boss should have sent her to Copper Lake instead of Liz. Joe wouldn't have been able to melt the first layer of permafrost that encased her if he tried.

Hell, Liz was hot-flashing just from seeing him. Just from *thinking* of him. And he wasn't trying to get a reaction from her.

"I'm listening, Mika."

"You're not supposed to be listening. You're supposed to be answering my question. Do you believe Joe Saldana when he says he doesn't know where his brother is?"

She wanted to think that he was well and truly done with Josh for at least the next fifteen years to life. After all, Josh was as big on screwing up as Joe was on responsibility.

On the other hand, they were identical twins. They'd shared their mother's womb, had the same face, the same eyes, the same DNA. Was breaking that bond permanently even possible?

"I don't know," she said. "He sounds sincere."

Mika voiced what Liz was thinking. "Don't all good liars?"

They did. As far as anyone knew, Joe was an honest law-abiding man, but most honest law-abiding people would lie for the right reason. Look at her. Lying was a big part of her job, and she sounded damn sincere when she did it. And Joe had spent half a lifetime with a brother who lied as easily as he breathed.

"My instincts say he or his parents are our best shot," she said. "It's always been Josh's pattern. When he screws up badly enough, he turns to his family for help."

"We're keeping tabs on the elder Saldanas as well. If Josh contacts them or shows up there, we'll know."

There was a murmur in the background on Mika's end. While she spoke to whoever had interrupted, Liz continued to gaze out the window. She wouldn't have heard the whirring of tires on sidewalk if they'd been talking, but she still would have known Joe had arrived home. Her stomach muscles tightening and the hair on the back of her neck standing on end were her usual reactions to danger, always sensed before seen.

He came into view through the window, coasting, one long muscular leg extended as he made the sharp turn to his house. He swung off the bike, then hefted it into the air and carried it up the steps to the porch. As he unlocked the door, he glanced toward Natalia's cottage, then right toward Pete's, but he didn't look over his shoulder at Liz's. Instead, he went inside, wheeling the bike with him, and closed the door.

Across the small lawn, the door shut with a sense of finality. Liz imagined she could even hear the lock clicking, securely shutting out the world for the night.

"Sorry about that," Mika said, returning her attention to Liz. "The wiretaps haven't provided anything of interest. Joe Saldana has renewed his membership in a group supporting green business practices. He's agreed to help coach a baseball team made up of six-year-olds and he's going to spend a small fortune taking two strays to the vet, where, at the appropriate time, of course, he'll spend another one getting them fixed. Oh, yes, and he's trying a new blend of coffee handpicked by gnomes on the northwest side of a volcanic Peruvian mountain only under a full moon and, therefore, commanding the price of a gazillion dollars per pound."

Liz grinned. Mika's sense of humor appeared so seldom that she regularly forgot the woman had one. "Trust me, if it's half as good as the stuff I've already had in his shop, it's worth every dime. Besides, gnomes don't work cheap, you know."

"Fortunately for America, we do." Mika's customary sobriety returned. "Other than calls to his parents, he has little contact with anyone outside the coffee shop. Since we got the wiretap order, he hasn't made or received a single call on his home phone. Ninety-five percent of his cell phone use is business-related, and ninety-five percent of the calls made to or from the shop are boyfriend-related."

"Esther has a boyfriend?" Liz imagined the waitress first with a boy barely old enough to be legal, then with a man more her age with the same wrinkles, the same orange hair. Neither was an appealing image.

"Not Esther. Raven." If Mika had been given to grimacing, Liz was sure she would have been doing so at the moment. "God save us from young love."

"Better that you guys hear it than me." What was Joe doing over there? Getting something to eat? Popping the top on a beer? Stripping off his clothes to take a shower?

Better not go there.

But it was too late to block the image of a long, lean body, of bare, tanned skin, wet hair slicked back as pounding water turned it dark gold.

It had been too late for them from the first time she'd seen him. Even if she weren't working, even if he weren't a subject in an investigation, Josh and her lies would always be between them.

"The trial is approaching quickly," Mika said. "If we don't have Josh Saldana in custody in time, the last two years will have been for nothing."

"Hey, that's two years of my life you're talking about." But Liz knew she was right. The U.S. Attorney might get a conviction anyway, at least on some of the charges, or the Mulroneys could walk.

There was a moment's silence before Mika spoke again. "Do you think they paid him off?"

It wasn't the first time they'd discussed the question. There was no doubt in anyone's mind that Josh could be bought, and probably pretty cheaply. If he'd had a chance to escape protective custody, avoid the trial *and* make some money doing it, he would have taken it. To hell with justice. To hell with the fact that the Mulroneys had tried to kill him, and had almost killed his brother. All Josh cared about was Josh.

"No," Liz said flatly. If he'd been bought off, then it meant someone in the marshals service or the U.S. Attorney's office had been involved. His location had been a well-kept secret. He'd gotten no phone calls or mail; he'd had zero contact with anyone outside their two offices. Only an insider could have acted as a go-between for the Mulroneys, and there was no evidence to suggest that.

Still, when your life was in other people's hands, as hers and Mika's had too often been, you couldn't help but wonder…

"Then he's probably run through whatever resources he might have had. Mom and Dad and little brother Joe are his last hope."

"If he can find them."

"They're keeping a low profile, but they're not exactly under the radar. The extended family knows where they are, and while they've denied any contact with Josh, we can't know whether they're telling the truth."

Again, Liz knew Mika was right. The Saldanas had relocated, not gone into hiding. They were using their own names, and Joe was in business for himself. It might take a bit of effort, but people like Josh were willing to expend a great deal of effort to avoid being responsible for themselves.

"I'll be in touch."

Before Liz could respond, Mika ended the call. No prolonged goodbyes for her. Heaven forbid Liz get the idea that she actually cared.

Then a flickering light came on in the lavender house—a television throwing shadows in Joe's otherwise-dark living room. Not caring, in that moment, seemed a damn good idea.

Forties' standards played on the café's stereo Thursday morning, Esther's music of choice. Even though she'd left half an hour earlier, Joe was letting the CD play out. The old tunes were comfortable, reminding him of his grandmother, who'd thought music began with Louis Armstrong and ended with Ella Fitzgerald. As kids, he and Josh had spent a lot of weekends at her house, taking turns dancing her around the table after Saturday night dinner while she'd told them stories of the grandfather they'd never known.

It was eleven o'clock, too late for mid-morning coffee breaks, too early for people making a java run at lunch. He'd had ten minutes since the last customer and caught up on everything that needed doing up front. He could head into his office, a small corner of the backroom, and do some paperwork, but the idea didn't move him from his spot leaning against the counter.

There was always time for paperwork, and always paperwork to be done.

He hated to admit it, but he'd thought Liz would come by this morning. Even during the busiest moments of their a.m. rush, when Esther liked to complain that they met themselves coming and going, his gaze had kept sliding to the door and the streets outside, expecting to catch a glimpse of black curls and amazing legs.

All morning he'd waited, and she hadn't come.

Scowling, he pushed away from the counter and took four steps toward the storeroom. Just as he reached it the sound of the doorbell made him pivot and return to the counter.

Not Liz. Just a stranger, tall, with a hard set to his features and even harder eyes. His gray suit was well-made but stark, the shirt a shade lighter, the tie a shade darker. He rocked back on his heels at the counter and studied the menu board posted on the wall above, skimming over the usual whipped, blended and frozen drinks. "Medium chai tea," he ordered in a voice as tough as his face.

"For here or to go?" Joe asked, suppressing a grin. Sure, chai tea was popular with his customers—his female customers. Pregnancy made Ellie crave it at least twice a day. But from a guy who looked as if he should be ordering coffee beans—*Don't need no cup. I'll just grind 'em in my mouth with a little hot water*—it was a surprise.

"Here."

Joe rang it up, made change for a twenty, then started the tea. Instead of taking a seat, the man stayed where he was, unmoving but giving the impression of loose energy, barely controlled.

"Nice town."

Breathing in steam fragrant with nutmeg and cloves, Joe glanced over his shoulder at the guy, and the hair on his nape automatically prickled. There was no reason for it, he told himself. So the guy wasn't a local, or even a good ol' Georgia boy. Not with that accent—New York, maybe New Jersey, blunted by years elsewhere. He waited on strangers all the time with all kinds of accents. It didn't mean anything.

"We like it," he said, sliding the porcelain mug across the counter.

"Nice change from the city."

Another prickle of unease slid down Joe's spine, but he kept his tone as steady as his hands. "Depends on the city." He had liked Chicago. Like his parents, he'd intended to spend the rest of his life there. He'd just needed a *different* place for a while.

"Chicago," the man replied with a humorless smile. "My name's Tom Smith, and Chicago's my kind of town."

Joe's hands weren't steady any longer. Where was a cop when you wanted him? Maricci, Decker, Petrovski…hell, he would have settled for a meter maid. Or a pregnant Ellie, or Esther breezing in because she'd forgotten something.

He was overreacting. A lot of people liked Chicago. It didn't mean Tom Smith was from there. It damn well didn't mean he knew the Mulroney brothers. He was just passing through, looking for decent chai tea, not an easy to thing to find in Copper Lake. So what if he looked like he might grace some most-wanted list, or dressed like a guy who might work for the Mulroneys? The best-dressed thugs in the world, Josh used to say. The one who'd shot *him* had been wearing Armani. Joe had recognized it because the same designer label had filled his own closet.

Joe shifted his gaze outside. It was an odd moment when he could look out the window and not see a single friend, but the people he saw now were only vague acquaintances or, in the case of Louise Wetherby, striding past with an armload of shopping bags, even less preferable than the man watching him.

"Do you miss it?" Smith asked.

"Miss what?"

"Your old hometown."

Joe straightened his shoulders and folded his arms across his chest. It was the middle of the day in downtown Copper Lake. Huge plate glass windows offered clear views into the shop. He had steaming pots of coffee within reach. Failing all that, the storeroom, with a decent lock, was only a few steps behind him, and a few steps past that was the outside door. And all that bike riding had given him leg muscles a track star would envy.

Run, he thought, and of course, he immediately thought of Josh, too. That was what he had always done. Run and let someone else deal with the fallout.

Pretending nonchalance, Joe shook his head. "I wouldn't mind going up for a game."

"Or a proper pizza."

"I'm partial to hot dogs myself. But this is a sweet place. It's got everything I want. If I feel the need for traffic and crowds, I can always go to Atlanta."

"Except your folks. They're not here."

Despite the heat radiating from the coffee pots, ice swept through Joe. So it was no coincidence Smith was here. No more pretence. "Leave my parents out of this."

Smith took a long, spice-flavored sniff of his tea and murmured appreciatively. "I'm not interested in your parents. I just want to find your brother."

"Why?"

"The same reason as everyone else." He drank the tea, then blotted his mouth with a napkin. "That was a tough thing—the mistaken identity bit. The Mulroneys didn't even know Josh had a brother, much less a twin. And there you were, walking out of his apartment, getting into his car." He shook his head sympathetically.

Can I borrow your car, Joe? We've got a hot date tonight. We're going someplace special for my birthday.

Joe's mind had fired in a dozen different directions. A serious date? In the weeks since Josh had introduced him to Liz, they hadn't had one real date, mostly just takeout at home. And someplace special? And Josh wanted to use Joe's Infiniti, wanted to return it to him smelling of her perfume, her shampoo, her everything.

Your birthday's not for two more months, he'd said sullenly.

Yeah, but she don't know that. Wink, wink, grin.

Joe had wanted to smash his fist into that grin. Instead, he'd traded car keys and walked out. Sixty seconds later, as he'd clicked the remote to unlock the door to Josh's truck, a man in a black overcoat had approached and shot him twice in the chest.

Maybe this man? Joe looked closer at Tom Smith. He couldn't say. The bastard had almost killed him, and he hadn't seen a thing besides the coat. Height, weight, hair color, eye color, skin tone—he hadn't had a clue. But he'd noticed the coat was Armani.

"It was a tough thing," Joe agreed. "You can probably understand when I say that because of it, Josh isn't particularly welcome around here. I'm all out of help to give him."

"If he shows up, you want to make a call, you could make some money."

"A reward for turning my brother in to people who want him dead?"

Smith gave him a long look, then reached slowly into his breast pocket and removed a silver card case. "The Mulroneys' reward is bigger than ours," he said as he slid a card out, then laid it on the counter between them. "But we, at least, can guarantee that we're not going to kill him."

Joe stared at the card but didn't pick it up. Engraved on the left side was the Department of Justice seal and on the other was contact information: Thomas P. Smith, U.S. Attorney's Office, Chicago, Illinois.

"We're pretty well-dressed thugs, too, Mr. Saldana," Smith said with a thin smile. "Or so your brother said."

Heat warmed Joe's cheeks—from standing too close to the coffee machines, of course. He turned away, fixed himself a cup of ice water and took a long drink before facing Smith again. "I haven't had any contact with him since the shooting. He doesn't even know where I am."

"We need him at the trial, Mr. Saldana. The government has put a lot into this case and we don't want to lose it because of him. We want to find him before the Mulroneys do."

"If you can't find him, how could they?"

Smith managed what Joe suspected was, for him, a smile, and his voice turned very dry. "They have resources we don't."

Joe left the card where it lay. "If you share any resources with them, tell them to stay the hell away from my parents and me. We won't help them and can't help you."

"If they find Josh first, they will kill him."

"Then maybe he'll have the good sense to stay lost." But even as he said it, Joe knew it wasn't likely. Josh had a bad habit of relying on family and friends. He was willing to take care of himself for only so long, and the two months since he'd left Liz had already exceeded that limit. He was probably looking for Joe and their parents, and Liz, and the woman he'd dated before her, and the woman before *her,* at that very moment.

"If your brother lacks one thing in great abundance, it's sense." Smith finished the tea, then set the mug on the counter. "My cell number's on the back of that card. If you change your mind—" Breaking off at Joe's scowl, he rephrased. "If you hear from Josh, let me know. We can protect him."

"Not from himself," Joe muttered. And hadn't Josh always been his own worst enemy?

Smith walked to the door before turning back. "Good tea. The cinnamon and cardamom were just right."

"I'll tell my taste tester." Ellie would be pleased, but she was used to compliments on her taste. It was what made her restaurant one of the most popular in town.

As Smith got into a black rental, the bell rang again and Natalia stopped in the doorway. "Can we come in?" Twisting around her ankles on leashes were the hellhounds, both straining to venture farther inside. A new place with new smells and all new things to pee on.

"I think health department regulations prohibit it, and I'm sure my own rules do. But I'll come out." Sliding the business card from the stainless steel counter, he crossed the dining room in a few strides and stepped out into muggy warmth and an excited, eight-legged greeting.

Natalia untangled long enough to hand him one leash, then sat on the bench a few feet away. The striped awning overhead protected it from too much sun and the worst of the rain when it came, and it had an unobstructed view of the cars driving by. There was no sign of Tom Smith's black rental.

Or Liz's red one.

"Are you going to name these guys?" Natalia asked as the fuzzy one jumped onto the bench between them, rolled onto his back and splayed all four legs in the air with a noticeable lack of dignity while she dutifully scratched his belly. The female was too busy sniffing every inch of Joe to notice.

"They don't respond to anything I call them."

"'Bad dog' and 'devil dog' don't count. They need proper names."

"How about Goldie and Brownie?"

Natalia rolled her eyes. This morning they were violet. "Would you answer to Blondie?"

"For the right person," he retorted, and an image of Liz popped into his mind. Damn it.

"How about Bear for this one?" Natalia gazed down at the fuzzy pup with more affection than she'd shown even Joe, and he was her best—maybe only—friend in town. "My mom used to sing a rhyme when I was little: 'Fuzzy wuzzy was a bear. Fuzzy wuzzy had no hair…'" Her voice grew softer with each word until it trailed away, as if the memory were so burdened with emotion that she could no longer sustain it. It was, Joe realized, the first truly personal thing she'd ever told him.

He swallowed the curiosity, and the lump in his throat, and the urge to wrap his arm around her, the way he used to do with his younger girl cousins when they were kids. "Okay. Bear it is. So can I still call this one Bad Dog?"

Natalia continued to stare off into the distance for a moment, then drew herself together. She shook her head, straightened her shoulders and erased the emotion from her eyes. "No, you can't. She's very regal. You could call her Princess."

"Or Queen Bitch."

"Naming a pet is like naming a child. You have to choose a name you won't be embarrassed to yell out the door."

"I wouldn't be embarrassed yelling Bad Dog or Queen Bitch," he grumbled. "Neither would she. She's probably proud of being both."

The female ran to sniff a piece of trash that had blown against the curb, and Joe reeled her back in, winning in spite of her valiant effort to resist. Immediately, she turned, her nose quivering, and locked in on the business card he was tapping against his thigh.

Natalia's gaze zeroed in on it, too. "U.S. Attorney's office?" She stared at him. "Are you in trouble?"

He tilted his head to mimic her position. "How can you read

that from there? Or have you seen so many U.S. Attorney's office business cards that you recognize them on sight?"

"My distance vision is very good. Are you in trouble?" she repeated.

If he avoided answering again, she would let him, but she was his best—though not only—friend in town, so he responded. "Not me, but someone I know."

"Your brother?"

"Yeah." He'd told her he had a brother in one of those early getting-acquainted conversations, but that had been the extent of it. He hadn't wanted to even think about Josh—about the hostility and the anger and the bitterness and the disappointment—much less talk about him. She'd had the same reaction to discussing her family: mother, father, two sisters, hadn't seen them in ages. He hadn't pressed, and neither had she.

"Is he in jail?"

"Not that I know of." Not yet.

"Where does he live?"

"Don't know that either."

"When was the last time you saw him?"

"It's been a while." He shot her a look. "Any more questions and you're gonna have to answer the same about your sisters."

That shut her up. She nudged the newly named Bear to the ground, then took the brown dog's leash from him. "We're going to head back home. I don't want to wind up carrying Bear the last block like I did last night."

Teasing her would be too easy, especially when she was serious, so Joe settled for shaking his head. He watched until they turned the corner before chuckling at the image of the fuzzy puppy cradled in Natalia's arms while the female darted and sniffed until she quivered.

"You're in a good mood."

Deliberately he lowered his gaze as he turned his head to

the right, seeing sidewalk, that bit of trash and a set of delicate feet with dark red-tipped toes. A vee of tan leather was anchored between the first and second toes, thin, intricately knotted as it stretched back to encircle slender ankles. A coral silk flower sat on the outside strap, just below the ankle bone, and the heels rose, lethally tall and thin.

As if the shoes weren't enough, they led to her legs, longer today, or so it seemed. Fact was, her dress was just so much shorter. Not indecently short, not even modesty-at-risk short. Just enticingly so.

"Moods can change." He finally managed to slide his gaze up over the snug-fitting dress that matched the silk flowers to her face. Her hair was down today, curls skewing in every direction. One fell across her forehead, and for an instant the temptation to brush it back was so strong that he actually lifted his hand to do so.

Silently swearing, he clenched his fist, and Tom Smith's business card crumpled inside it. He surged to his feet, scooped up the trash from the curb, then reached the shop door in two steps.

"Don't hurry off on my account."

"This isn't hurrying. It's me getting back to work."

She made a show of peering through the glass. "I don't see any customers."

He had the door open. All he had to do was walk through and let it close. Maybe she would follow, maybe she wouldn't. He didn't have to look at her again and he damn sure didn't have to say anything else. But he held the door open and he did both.

"Why don't you be the next one, then?"

Chapter 4

Liz would bet that piece of paper had blown at least a block. Cars had driven over it, people had stepped on it, but only Joe had bothered to pick it up and put it in the trash.

Switching her shoulder bag to her other arm, she reached for the door he held open, then followed him inside. The purse was smaller than she normally carried, but her GLOCK didn't fit inside just any old bag. She ordered a frozen hazelnut coffee blend with extra whipped cream as she slipped her debit card from the pocket next to the .45.

Joe waved the card away, but she insisted. "If you want to make me coffee at home for free, I'll accept, but not here."

"Consider it a sample."

"I've already had a sample and I liked it," she pointed out, and just that quickly, the air turned hot and heavy. She was in sorry shape when a truly innocent comment could raise her blood pressure and her core temperature into the danger zone.

Judging by the intensity of his stare, he was in equally sorry shape.

After he swiped her card, she went to a table, sat down and crossed her legs. Her foot bobbed in the air, displaying her to-die-for sandal at its best. She'd learned on her first job to use the tools she had, and with Joe, she was well aware, that included her legs.

He brought her drink to the table, along with a glass of water for himself. "How do you walk in those things?"

She stretched out her leg, tilting her foot from side to side. "Rather gracefully, I think. Don't you?"

"I wasn't watching." He pulled out the chair across from her and sprawled in it.

Liar. Liz sipped the coffee drink and practically hummed with satisfaction. "Whoever invented frozen coffee was a genius. It's even better than ice cream."

"Better than sex."

She took a long sip, her gaze locked on him, then shook her head. "If you think that, you've been sleeping with the wrong women."

Pink tinged his cheeks even as he frowned at her. A grown man who still blushed. How cool was that?

"That's the name of a drink at this little shop I used to go to in Chicago," he explained. "Coffee, ice cream, hazelnut, chocolate—I don't know what all went into it. But it was pretty damn impressive."

"And you haven't tried to duplicate it?"

"It was their creation, not mine." He gestured out the window. "You just missed Natalia and the dogs."

"I saw them drag her around the corner. She's a very good friend to take care of them for you."

Joe snorted. "She's the one who brought them home. It's only fair that she share the responsibility."

Liz used the tip of the straw to scoop some whipped cream off the top of her drink. "I heard you calling them last night. Bad Dog? Worse Dog? You should be ashamed of yourself. They need proper names."

"They have names. The fuzzy one's Bear, and the female… We decided she's rather regal. You know, queen of all she surveys, so she needed a queenly name." Humor glinted in his blue eyes. "I chose Elizabeth."

"Elizabeth," she repeated.

"It was either that or Latifah, and she doesn't look like a Latifah to me. Elizabeth just seems to fit her."

"So…" She took a long moment to lick every bit of whipped cream off the straw—too long if the sudden paleness that crept into his face was any indication. "Is there supposed to be some subtle message in naming your dog after me? Like, oh, I don't know…that we're both bitches?"

He looked far too innocent for any male over the age of ten, especially one who'd grown up since the womb with Josh Saldana. "I would never call you that."

"But you might think it." He shrugged, and she laughed. "I've had worse insults than having a dog named after me. Besides, your Elizabeth is pretty, runs you ragged and is totally beyond your control. Sounds good to me."

"That's what they make dog trainers and crates for—to put her completely under my control."

It was Liz who snorted this time. "Not that one. For a puppy, she has a very strong sense of self. It'll be easier for you to bend to her will than to bend her to yours."

"Probably so." He rested his head against the window behind him, eyes closed. "Like it would be easier to tell you where Josh is than to convince you I don't know."

Her gut clenched and her hand developed a fine tremor. Excitement, she told herself, because the last couple months' work might pay off. Not disappointment at all. Hadn't she told Mika that she didn't believe Joe's claim about not knowing where Josh was? Hadn't she thought he was lying?

But thinking and knowing were two different things.

With her pleasure in the coffee gone, she set the cup on the table. "So you do know."

He opened one eye to look at her, then both. His gaze was steady, nothing in its blue depths. No guilt, no regret, no shame. Just a cool, even, unwavering look. "No, I don't."

"But you said—"

He shook his head. "It would be easier to lie to you than to convince you that I'm not lying."

Relief and irritation and the faint niggling suspicion that he was still lying made her scowl. "Do you really expect me to believe that your identical twin brother who has relied on you to save his ass all your lives hasn't been in touch with you for more than two years?"

The bell announced two customers, and he glanced their way, greeting them with a nod, before turning his attention back to her. "See, that's the problem, Liz." He stood, scooted the chair back up to the table and picked up his glass before he leaned close. "I don't care what you believe."

She breathed in, catching a whiff of his cologne beneath the scent of sweetened coffee, and resorted to a shallower, insufficient breath as he walked away. He moved easily, comfortably, giving no hint to his customers that he had recently been the least bit flustered.

Proved he was a good liar, didn't it?

Business picked up, giving Joe a legitimate reason to keep his distance from her. She finished her drink and considered ordering another, weighing a few more minutes of coffee heaven against the workout required to keep the calories from going straight to her hips, and regretfully decided against it.

Instead, she stood, left a tip anchored under the cup, and strolled across the dining room to the door, outside onto the sidewalk and out of sight.

When Liz got home, Mrs. Wyndham was kneeling near the flower beds that marked the border between the main house and the cottages. Shading her eyes against the sun in spite of the floppy hat she wore, she gave Liz half a second to get out of the car, then called to her. "Don't you look pretty today?"

"Why, thank you, Mrs. Wyndham." Liz headed her way, pausing to kick off her shoes once she reached the grass. As she passed the pink cottage, movement inside caught her eye—a shadow at the screen door, flanked by two smaller shadows. She wiggled her fingers in greeting, though she couldn't see if Natalia responded.

The color surrounding the old lady was provided by flats of flowers awaiting planting, at least a dozen or more. Wiggling her toes in the lush, sun-warmed grass, Liz said, "You've got almost enough flowers here to make my mother happy."

"Is your mother a gardener?"

"Only part-time, but she has a very green thumb, which I didn't inherit. I'm lucky to keep a cactus alive."

"I don't believe in green thumbs," Mrs. Wyndham said seriously. "Gardening is a science. Plants have certain requirements, and if you meet them, they flourish. If you don't, they die."

"Oh, but it's an art, too. Shaping the beds, mixing colors, knowing what looks good where…and you're a master artist, Mrs. Wyndham."

"I'd better be. I'm one of the cofounders of the horticultural society in town." Removing one dirt-encrusted glove, the old lady lifted a flat of zinnias from a cart that doubled as a bench and shoved it in her direction. "How's Joe?"

Liz obediently sat, laying her shoes on the grass beside her. "The last time I saw him, he was fine."

"That's what all the girls think. They all like him, but you know, I can't recall him going out on a single date the whole time he's lived here. He danced once with Sophy Marchand at the Halloween festival last year, but I think that's as far as it went. You don't suppose he's gay, do you?"

If Liz had been standing in her heels, she would have toppled out of them. "No," she said hastily, breathlessly. Then she gave herself a mental shake. "Not dating doesn't mean a person doesn't like the opposite sex. I mean, I like guys, but I don't date much. It's been more than two years since I went out with anyone."

Mrs. Wyndham's hands stilled, a clump of yellow-and-orange lantana dangling from them, and she fixed her gaze on Liz. "That's a shame. Did he break your heart?"

"Who?"

"Joe. It's obvious, isn't it? You two used to know each other, he's been here nearly two years and hasn't gone out with a single woman, you haven't gone out with another man in two years, you come looking for him…"

"No," Liz said with a bit too much emphasis even to her own ears. "The timing is just coincidence. We weren't involved."

Who was lying now? That night in Josh's kitchen… She'd been cleaning up after dinner; Joe had come in to get a beer. She had just shut off the lights and turned, and there he was, near and handsome and strong and decent and everything his brother wasn't. And the sizzle… Damn that sizzle. From the first time they'd met, it had been there, skipping along her veins, dancing upon her nerves, tempting her to forget her job and her case and everything she was for just the chance, the smallest chance, to explore the attraction to him.

They'd stood there in the dimly lit room, everything else faded, mere inches from touching, and everything in her had *ached* for that touch. She'd wanted it so much and so badly, and so had he; she'd seen it in his face, had felt it in the tension radiating off him in waves. It had taken every bit of strength she possessed to remember why they couldn't have that touch.

Remember Josh.

The words had been for herself, but they'd had the right effect on Joe. He'd looked stunned.

And an instant later, Josh had barged down the hall.

"Tommy—that's my grandnephew by marriage—he's a detective for the local police—says there's no such thing as coincidence." Finally, Mrs. Wyndham plunged the lantana into the soft dirt and patted the soil around it.

In the moment the woman's attention was on the plant, Liz seized the opportunity to send the conversation on a tangent. "I thought maybe Joe and Natalia were involved."

Mrs. Wyndham pursed her lips in thought. "I don't think so. I think she's more like the sister he never had. She's an odd girl. I never met anyone who seemed more alone. I don't even know why she stays here. She keeps to herself except for Joe. And now she's brought home those strays. I think she identifies with them. Someone threw them out, and someone threw her out, and now Joe's taking care of all three of them."

Liz resisted the urge to point out that, so far, Natalia had done most of the taking care of the dogs. Joe had bought food and given them a place to spend the night, but Natalia did the actual feeding, the walking, the playing, the loving.

"Where is she from?" Liz asked instead.

"She's never said." Mrs. Wyndham pulled another clump of lantana from the plastic flat and dug a hole for it a few inches from the first.

"I don't use typical standards for renting the cottages," Mrs. Wyndham went on. "I don't ask for driver's licenses or credit or personal references. I've known Pete all his life.

Credit references couldn't tell me anything about him that I don't already know. And Joe…well, you can just look at Joe and know that he's a good guy. Everyone in town adores him. Half of his friends are cops or lawyers, the churchy people like him a lot and the kids love him."

Liz thought of the pictures of Josh loaded on her computer. Using Mrs. Wyndham's logic, he would appear to be a good guy, too. After all, he shared Joe's trust-inspiring face, and was charming, as well. He could charm their socks right off, and steal their shoes for good measure.

"Joe tells me Natalia needs a place to stay, he vouches for her, and I say sure. Any friend of Joe's…" The woman flashed her a smile that made her feel about six inches tall. Apparently, Joe hadn't yet told their landlord that Liz was no friend of his. She'd lied, and he'd let her. Because he'd thought she needed a place to stay? Because he'd thought Josh had let her down and she needed someone to take care of her, like Natalia and the puppies?

She would prefer that Joe think of her differently than Natalia. She'd really prefer that he not consider her a stray like the puppy who now shared her name. She was strong. She had a good job. She'd spent two years taking care of herself and his worthless brother.

"Does he ever have visitors from out of town?"

"Not that I've noticed, though he does borrow my car on occasion to go somewhere."

"Where?" To Savannah to visit his parents? Mika had mentioned that he called them regularly, but she hadn't said anything about him showing up in person.

"Just day trips that he can't make on his bike. He always returns it to me washed and with a full tank of gas. And when I ask if he enjoyed himself, he always says he had a very good time. Maybe he's got a girlfriend we don't know about." Mrs.

Wyndham's shrewd gaze turned on Liz. "Was he visiting you before you came here?"

"No." It was likely his parents. They'd always been close. It was reasonable that he'd want to see them as often as he could.

"That would certainly explain why he's never shown any interest in the women around here," Mrs. Wyndham mused. "Because his sweetheart in Atlanta or Augusta or wherever already has claims on him."

It was possible, Liz grudgingly admitted as she mumbled something about the time, grabbed her shoes and headed for the cottage. Joe was a grown man who'd led an active life in Chicago, professionally and personally. There was no way that getting shot would make him swear off women. According to reports, a stream of them had visited him during his recovery in the hospital, all sympathetic, all wanting to take care of him. He probably did have a girlfriend somewhere, and it didn't matter to her.

As soon as she stepped inside the house, she flung one shoe across the room so hard that it clattered and skidded until the kitchen cabinets stopped it.

It didn't matter to her in the least.

The clock on the coffee shop wall was just shy of nine by the time Joe began shutting off lights. He'd been about to walk out the door nearly three hours earlier when Raven had pleaded for the evening off so she could go to a concert in Augusta with the "awesome guy" who'd transformed her into a normal-looking teenage girl. Figuring she could do normal only for a week, maybe two max, then the boy would probably move on, he let her go. Fifteen hours on the job wasn't so bad. He'd done it for months when he first opened the place.

He slid the bank deposit into his backpack, then wheeled the bike into the alley, stopping long enough to secure the door. The bank was only two blocks south. It wouldn't add more than a couple minutes to his ride home.

He crossed onto Oglethorpe, coasting, listening to the sounds of customers leaving Ellie's Deli at the other end of the block. The night was cool, the humidity low, barely noticeable. Whatever he missed about Chicago, he loved the Georgia nights.

He was passing the square when a familiar noise came from the shadows of the park: half bark, half demanding yip. He heard it each night when he forced Bad Do—Elizabeth—back inside after her last trip out, when he moved her from his spot on the couch or his side of the bed and again when he disturbed her sleep when he got up in the morning. Maybe, if he was lucky, she'd escaped Natalia and found a new owner who couldn't bear to return her.

"Elizabeth," a voice admonished from the dark. "Play nice, or I won't take you for a walk again."

He wasn't that lucky.

Small feet scrabbled across the walkway, then the dog appeared through a break in the bushes. Dragging Liz behind, she darted toward him, forcing him to steer sharply away to avoid her, nearly losing his balance. She didn't look the least bit repentant when he righted himself and the bike, but jumped up, front paws muddying his jeans, and started licking him.

"Oh, look, Elizabeth, it's Daddy," Liz said sweetly as she reeled in the extra-long leash.

He scowled as he pushed the dog away. "What are you two doing out here?"

"We're working off a little excess energy."

"Where's Natalia?"

"She was with us, but Bear doesn't have Elizabeth's stamina. She had to take him back."

"Was she carrying him again?"

"Not when we split, but I think she was just waiting for us to get out of sight before she picked him up."

"God, she's a sucker."

"She's just got a soft place in her heart for Bear." Liz reined in the puppy a little more, then smiled. "I think I'm developing a soft spot for this one. We have so much in common."

Yeah, he could think of a few things. He kept them to himself, though. "I don't think you've burned up enough energy. She's still pretty wired."

"I imagine she stays wired even in her sleep. Where are you headed?"

"Bank." He nodded toward the red-white-and-blue sign for Fidelity Mutual. When she and Elizabeth turned that way, he swung his leg over the bike frame, removed his helmet and hung it from the handlebars, then began pushing it one-handed alongside the curb.

"Long day, huh?"

"Yeah." Funny, though, he didn't feel as tired as he had ten minutes ago. What was that about?

"Mine was leisurely. After brightening your morning, I went home and talked with Mrs. Wyndham while she planted a ton of flowers."

She was smiling broadly, the teasing smile of a woman who'd heard interesting things. But not about him. The last time he'd done anything interesting was when he'd gotten shot. In Copper Lake, he'd lived like a monk.

But because she was waiting for a response, and he didn't see any reason to disappoint her, he said, "You know Natalia isn't the only one who calls Mrs. Wyndham the old windbag."

"That's not nice. I found everything she had to say terribly interesting."

"Like what?"

"She thinks you collect strays. Natalia, the puppies, me."

She shrugged as if being considered his stray didn't bother her at all. While the thought of her being his *anything* bothered him a great deal. "And she wonders if you're gay."

He wasn't quite sure how to respond to that, but the laugh that escaped him settled it. "For the record, I'm not. And I'm not offended by her wondering."

"For the record, I didn't think you were. And I don't know if I expected you to be offended. A lot of men would be." She paused as the dog trotted off to thoroughly sniff an azalea. The nearest streetlamp cast yellow-tinged light over Liz's curls and gave her white T-shirt a faint matching hue. The shirt clung to her curves and ended at her waist, an inch above her khaki shorts. Heavy green tennis shoes should have looked clunky, but instead they emphasized the lean muscles of her calves.

Keep your mind on the conversation—Mrs. Wyndham, you, gay. "My college roommate was gay. We stayed in touch until I came here. He's smart, successful, has great clothes, has been in the same relationship for ten years and started a family a few years ago by adopting a little girl. What's offensive about being compared to him?"

"Living with him didn't make you uncomfortable?"

He snorted. "I'd lived with Josh for eighteen years. That was a hell of a lot more uncomfortable. God only knew what he might do."

"Like cause you to lose touch with your roommate and the rest of your friends."

Finally the dog began moving again, and within a minute or two of silence, they reached the bank. He dropped the locked bag into the night slot, then gazed around. Home was to the northeast. Nearer, only a block to the west, was the SnoCap Drive-In, a fifties-era joint with greasy burgers, crispy fries and home-brewed root beer. "Have you had dinner?"

"I have, but I'd like something cold to drink."

He gestured, and they headed toward the corner. Halfway there, he responded to her last real comment. "When I got out of the hospital, I followed Josh's lead. I ran away. I left Chicago as soon as I was able, I didn't tell anyone but Mom and Dad where I was going, and I haven't had any contact with anyone from there since. People here know where I came from, but they don't know why. In the beginning it was easier not to tell them, and now…" Now it was easier to just go with the status quo.

"You don't want them to know that you were the victim of a violent crime? Because it's not that uncommon."

"I know. It happens even here."

"So the victim of violence part doesn't bother you. Is it because your brother was involved? Or because…" Liz shortened the leash to pull Elizabeth back from the street, and her voice turned thoughtful. "You said you ran away. You think leaving Chicago was cowardly? That you should have stayed as if nothing had happened?"

They turned onto Carolina Avenue. The lights were brighter there, with the only traffic Joe had seen since leaving the shop. It was mostly kids in this part of town at night, cruising between the SnoCap, Charlie's Custom Rods next door and Taquito Taco on the west side of the river. A group of boys gathered around the raised hoods of cars older than they were in Charlie's parking lot, comparing one rumbling engine to the other, while newer cars filled most of the spaces at the SnoCap.

"I never got the car thing," Joe said as they cut through Charlie's lot and headed for the lone outside table at the drive-in. "Even when I was their age, a car was just transportation. As long as it got me where I was going, I didn't care about the rest."

"Oh, I don't know. I think that car you had in Chicago was more a status symbol than just transportation. You were successful and everything—the car, the clothes, the condo—showed it."

Joe grinned. "I do miss the suits sometimes. I looked damn good in Armani."

She tied Elizabeth's leash to a post a few feet away. "You look pretty damn good in jeans and T-shirts."

He stared at her. Her tone had been casual, but there was nothing casual about the heat that burned through him. She thought he looked good in his clothes, huh? Was she interested in seeing how he looked without them? Scars aside, that was good, too, and he was real damn interested in seeing her without her clothes.

Or he would be, if she hadn't been Josh's first.

If he knew for absolute certain that she wasn't still Josh's.

He parked his bike out of the dog's range before asking what she wanted.

"My pockets are empty except for keys. Buy me a diet cherry limeade, and it'll be my treat next time."

He went to the window, where one of his after-school regulars greeted him with a smile too warm and friendly for a girl half his age. "Hey, Joe. You want your usual?"

"Yeah, plus a large diet cherry limeade."

The girl—he remembered she ordered a tall caramel-drizzle frappucino every time but couldn't recall her name—looked past him to the table, and her glossy pink mouth settled into a pout. "I've never seen her before. Who is she?"

"Her name is Liz. She's…" His brother's ex-girlfriend? Maybe current? The woman he would have gladly gotten hot and dirty with if she hadn't said the magic words—*Remember Josh.* How the hell could he forget him? "She's new in town."

Caramel-drizzle—Carmie, that was her name—tossed her blond ponytail over her shoulder. "I hadn't heard you were seeing anyone."

"I hadn't either."

"So are you guys, what? Like, friends?"

He glanced over his shoulder at Liz, sitting now, with Elizabeth bracing her paws on her thigh. She was scratching the dog behind the ears, and the pup was quivering from the tip of her nose all the way down to her tail.

Joe imagined he might do the same if Liz got physical with him.

Tapping nails drew his attention back to Carmie, who was still pouting. "Yeah," he replied. Friends was as good a description as any.

With a disgruntled sound, Carmie turned away to fix their drinks, then set the cups in front of him and made change. "The food will be out in a minute."

He stifled the urge to offer to wait and returned to the table. Elizabeth immediately tried to climb into his lap, stopping only when Liz gave her a stern *No*.

"Teach me to do that," he said. "She's lived with me forty-eight hours and so far 'dinner' is the only word she's acknowledged."

"It's all a matter of attitude."

"Yeah. She's got it and I don't." He settled into the plastic chair, crossed one ankle over the other knee and gazed into the distance. If he'd shown up at Ellie's, Tia Maria's or Chantal's with Liz, the gossip would have spread across town by the time they got home. But none of these kids besides Carmie even noticed them, and she would have forgotten by the time she got home.

That was good. If people were going to gossip about him, he'd rather have them wondering if he was gay than what was between him and Liz.

Besides, of course, Josh.

"You never answered me." With one elegantly slender

hand, Liz gestured toward Charlie's. "On the way here, you called leaving Chicago 'running away.' Is that how you see it? How you see yourself? As a coward?"

He had hoped she would forget the question or at least give him the courtesy of pretending to forget. He'd never talked about this with anyone—not that he had many people to talk to. It wasn't exactly a topic he could bring up with his parents. Even the slightest reminder, and his dad teared up and his mom's behavior bordered on frantic: cleaning, blathering, even spontaneous bursts of prayer.

His muscles were so tense that it felt as if shrugging might make them crackle. "Thousands of people are victimized every year, and they don't pack up and run off to find someplace safer to live. They don't break with their past and start all over someplace new. They don't hide."

She took a long suck on her drink before giving her own more convincing shrug. "You didn't change your name or your appearance. You haven't isolated yourself in the back of beyond. You don't carry a gun or view everyone with suspicion. You have a business. You have friends and neighbors, and you've taken on new obligations. You go out at night. You talk to strangers. You're not in hiding."

"I'm not in Chicago either."

Another delicate wave of those fingers, this time dismissing his argument. "Staying in Chicago wouldn't have made you any stronger or braver. People there wanted your brother dead. Since you happen to look exactly like him, getting out was the smart thing to do, at least until those people are put in jail."

"Josh isn't going to make any effort to help with that, is he?" The bitterness was heavier in his voice than he'd intended. God knew, he felt a lot of resentment toward Josh, but he owed him at least a little fairness. If leaving town and staying away was the smart thing for Joe, then wasn't it doubly smart for Josh since he'd been the Mulroneys' target in the first place?

Carmie delivered his burger and fries, along with a handful of napkins and a long look for Liz, and the dog immediately returned to his side, greedily eyeing the food.

"Maybe he'll surprise everyone," Liz said as he handed a pinched-off piece of hamburger bun to the puppy. "Maybe his conscience will force him to appear for the trial."

Joe laughed, and the tension between his shoulders eased. "You've mistaken Josh for someone else. He doesn't *have* a conscience."

"He has one. He just doesn't listen to it very often." She pried the top off her cup, then fished out the cherry. "Do you intend to go back to Chicago once the trial is over?"

It was an easy answer, something he'd thought about and decided right after he'd moved to Copper Lake. But as he watched her dangle the cherry by its stem, raise it into the air, tilt her head back and open her mouth, all conscious thought left him. His mind went blank, his lungs burned for air, his skin heated and arousal rushed in his ears and through his body.

She closed her teeth around the cherry, pulled the stem loose, then chewed, making a soft *mmm* sound. Dots of sweat popped out on his forehead, and his hand was unsteady as he reached for his root beer, gulping half of it in one swallow.

"Is that a hard question?"

Question? Oh, yeah, Chicago. "No. I decided when I bought the shop that if I liked it here, I would stay."

"And you like it."

"I do." *And I'm liking it more every day.* "It's a different life."

"Quieter," she said with a nod.

"And slower."

"You work long hours."

"But I worked eighty-hour weeks in Chicago. I'm my own

boss now. I get to make the decisions." He chewed a bite of burger and swallowed slowly before continuing. "At the investment firm, I didn't remember the names of most of the people I worked with. I talked to my parents every couple days, but I hardly ever saw them. I scheduled time for dates and sex. My focus was on my career above everything else."

Like Josh's focus had been on himself.

Maybe they'd had more in common than just shared genes.

"And here your focus is on living a fuller life. Quality versus quantity. You don't have to schedule dating and sex anymore." She paused only long enough to grab a handful of Elizabeth's leash as the puppy stiffened when kids climbed out of a nearby car. "So why aren't you doing it?"

His throat required another gulp of root beer before he could speak, and then his voice was hoarse. "Having sex?"

"Actually, I meant dating," she said drily, "but the other's interesting, too. Are you doing *it?*"

If he'd been wearing a tie, as he had every day for years, he would have been choking on it. "None of your business."

"Mrs. Wyndham thinks you might be seeing a girlfriend when you borrow her car for out-of-town trips."

"I thought she wondered if I was gay."

Liz shook her head, her curls rippling. "The possibility occurred to her, and she was probably prepared to be very PC and accepting of it if it were true, but she'd prefer to think you've got a sweetheart somewhere. Do you?"

He polished off the last bit of his burger and crumpled the cold fries in the greasy wrapper. "I'll make you a deal, Liz. I'll tell you all about my sex life right after you tell me why you're looking for Josh."

For an instant, he thought, she looked tempted, as if one bit of information might be worth trading for the other. Then she shook her head, a wry smile curving her lips. "See, that's the problem," she said, parroting his words from earlier that day. "I don't care about your sex life."

For two years, neither had he. This was a hell of a time for things to change.

And a hell of a person to cause the change.

Chapter 5

Friday started out bright and sunny, but by mid-morning, the sky had turned dark. The wind picked up, bringing rain in a gentle fall, exactly what Mrs. Wyndham's newly planted flowers needed. Liz would have preferred a deluge. She would have kicked off her shoes, gone out into the grass and let it drench her, washing away the edginess and the attraction that was too damn close to becoming something more.

Important.

Real.

Something she didn't need, didn't want, wouldn't have.

Her windows were open, and she was sitting cross-legged on the sofa, the wicker creaking each time she moved. It was a comforting sound, already growing familiar after so short a time. With her laptop balanced on her knees, she checked her e-mail, let her mother know that she'd be home for a visit at the first opportunity, then signed off to face the photograph of Josh that served as wallpaper.

He and Joe were identical, right down to the gleam in their blue eyes and the tilt to their smiles, but she'd never had a problem telling them apart, though it hadn't been the obvious things like personal style. Josh had been cocky, sure of his appeal, comfortable in denim and leather, while Joe had been the poster boy for career success.

The difference for her had been simpler: Joe attracted her; Josh didn't.

Josh had been a job. Joe had been…

Off-limits, she reminded herself. And nothing had changed.

Her cell phone trilled, and she glanced at the screen before answering. "Hey, Mika."

"Are you enjoying the rain?"

Liz rolled her eyes. "Do you have the weather report for Copper Lake called up on your computer?"

"Yes, I do. It's one of the first things I see when I boot up. Seventy-four degrees and raining. Expected to clear by midnight, with sunshine tomorrow."

Another of the first things she saw on the computer, Liz suspected, was the same photograph of Josh that she herself was looking at. Mika's attention, first and foremost, was the case.

While Liz kept having trouble remembering it.

She closed the laptop screen, then set it on the coffee table. "You have anything new for me?"

"Not really. Thomas Smith arrived in Copper Lake yesterday. He made contact with Joe Saldana, who insisted he doesn't know his brother's whereabouts."

Liz had met Smith a few times before her team had removed Josh from Chicago. He appeared more organized crime than prosecutor, a seriously tough-looking guy…who'd attended Milton Academy and Yale before graduating from

Harvard Law. He was single, a little too smug for her tastes, and had informed her after one meeting that he would have asked her out if he didn't have a policy against dating feds. Mika, who'd been at the meeting, too, had given him the look that turned most men to stone, but he'd seemed not to notice. Unusual, because men always noticed Mika.

"He's staying in Atlanta a few days. One of our people in that office is going to pay Joe a visit. We think it will solidify your story if you're there at the time, so he'll coordinate with you first."

Oh, good. She so liked playing the role of clingy ex-girl-friend who didn't know when to leave well enough alone.

"Have you been inside his house?"

"Not yet."

"What are you waiting for?"

"Gee, I don't know. An invitation?" Rising from the sofa, Liz stretched, then padded to the open door. "Why don't you get a warrant?"

"We can do that, but since you're living fifty feet away…"

Stepping outside onto the porch, Liz gauged the distance between her cottage and Joe's. Probably no more than a few inches from fifty feet. Did Mika have a satellite photo of the cottages called up on her computer, too?

"Do you think he would just leave evidence lying around?"

"No," Mika conceded. "But law-abiding citizens tend to be clumsy in their attempts to protect their loved ones."

Liz wouldn't exactly describe Josh as Joe's loved one. He carried a lot of rancor toward his brother. But blood was thicker than water, family first, blah, blah, blah.

"I'll see how he feels about company this evening." It was the action Mika wanted, but it disturbed Liz because she wanted it, too. She would like to see how Joe lived. Was his cottage as bare as her own, or had he truly settled in? Was he messy, neat, in between? Did the lavender house bear any resemblance to the chilly condo where he'd lived in Chicago, furnished by an interior designer and hardly looking lived in?

She would be happier about it if she didn't have to worry. So far, their time together had been pretty public, but she'd still had erotic dreams last night. Alone? In his house? Good cause for concern.

"Let me know," Mika said. "And don't get too distracted."

"Distracted?" Liz echoed as she sat on the porch floor, the siding at her back.

"I know you had mixed feelings about going to Copper Lake." Mika hesitated. "I know you had mixed feelings about Joe."

Which was more astonishing? That Mika was actually getting personal? Or that she'd seen what Liz had been sure she'd kept very well hidden from everyone except Joe? "I don't know—"

"I was there when you visited him in the hospital."

Liz squeezed her eyes shut. Josh hadn't seen anything. His parents had been too grief-stricken to notice. Tom Smith hadn't said anything, and she was pretty sure he would have. Like Mika, his case came first.

"I'll stay focused," she said flatly.

"I'm sure you will. Call me."

"I'm sure I will," Liz mimicked after she pressed the End button. She flipped the phone shut with a defiant snap, then heaved a sigh. There were easier cases out there. If she could trade this one…

She wouldn't. She'd given too much time to it. She'd wound up handcuffed to her bed because of it. She would do her best to find Josh and persuade him to testify, and then she would return to life as normal. The Mulroneys would go to prison, Josh would be in trouble again before she made it home and Joe would know the truth. Would know she'd lied.

He would want only to forget, and she would always remember. And wonder.

The day passed slowly, the rain falling ceaselessly. At five, she changed into a short cotton skirt and a scoop-necked tank. She pinned back her curls and put on makeup, earrings and clunky clogs. Her minimal belongings didn't include an umbrella or a slicker, so after making a phone call, she tucked her cell into her bag, locked up and did the fifty-foot dash to Joe's porch.

There she shook her hair, thinking with a grin that Elizabeth and Bear, both barking now inside the house, would likely have the same reaction to the rain, then she kicked off her shoes. By the time Joe came around the corner at five-thirty, she was sitting in one of his rockers, legs stretched out, feet propped on the porch railing, damp clothes clinging to her skin.

He didn't notice her until he was halfway up the steps, bike gripped in both hands. He stopped abruptly and stared at her until something—maybe the weight of the bike or the rain in his face—made him move the last few feet to shelter.

"Hey." He set down the bike, then removed his helmet. His hair was dry, but it was likely the only part of him that was. His baby-blue T-shirt and jeans hugged him like a second skin, and water sluiced off to puddle at his feet.

The temperature had dropped enough to make wet clothing chilly, but he didn't look cold. She didn't feel it. Struggling to sound unaffected, she said, "If you had a car, you wouldn't have gotten so wet coming home."

"If I had a car, I'd be part of the problem, not the solution. Do you know how much pollution they put into the atmosphere?"

"Sometimes, though, a bicycle isn't a reasonable option."

"Sometimes. Some places. Copper Lake isn't one of those places."

He toed off each shoe, kicked them against the wall, then

stripped off his socks and stood there, barefooted like her. There was something incredibly appealing about the sight. Apparently unaware that she'd discovered an all-new fascination with bare feet, he said, "Make yourself comfortable."

"I am."

"I'm not."

"Probably because you need to get out of those clothes." The instant the last word was out, she swallowed hard. Wrong thing to say, very wrong thing to think about. Joe out of his clothes would be too tempting, and she was already feeling weak.

"Yeah, I guess I do," he said, but he didn't move toward the door.

"I hope you don't mind me inviting myself over, but I thought I'd repay you for the cherry limeade last night. I ordered two medium pizzas to be delivered in—" Rocking forward, she slid her fingers around his left hand and lifted it so she could see the face of his watch.

His skin was warm, not as soft as her own but not particularly callused either. His fingers tensed for just a moment, then went lax in her grip, and his pulse throbbed just the slightest bit harder. There was a small scar on the back of his hand, right where the blood vein was most prominent, reminding her of the time in the hospital when an IV had been taped there. When he'd looked so pale, so vulnerable and still so damn handsome.

"Delivered when?" His voice was husky, sliding over her skin, bringing back the sharp edginess that had plagued her earlier.

It took a few heartbeats to remember her reason for taking his hand. "Twenty minutes." Hers was husky, too. Edgy.

"What kind?"

"One vegetarian, one supreme."

"My favorite. But I should change first." He was waiting for her to release him, she realized belatedly when he tugged free. Taking a step back, he pulled his keys from his pocket, propped the screen with one foot and unlocked the door. Before opening it, he asked, "Do you want to come in?"

More than she wanted to admit even to herself—and less, too, because Mika had told her to get a look inside. She forced a breath and let the chair rock back with a squeak. "You just want me to deflect the puppies' attention from you."

His grin started out a bit shaky, but reached full-force as he twisted the doorknob. "You can't blame me for trying."

He opened the door just enough to squeeze through and the dogs' yips increased in volume, making it difficult to separate his words from the din. "Hey, Bear. Hey, Elizabeth. What did you guys destroy today?"

With a sigh, she settled back in the chair as a sound from the right broke the gentle patter of the rain. When she turned, her gaze connected with Natalia, standing motionless on her porch. The younger woman's expression was utterly blank. If she was jealous or resentful or feeling a little hostile, she hid it well.

She pivoted as if to return inside, prompting Liz to speak. "Hey, we're having pizza. Want to join us?" There was nothing like a third person to keep things from getting too intimate, a lesson she and Joe had learned once before. She should have thought of it sooner.

"No, thanks. I don't like pizza."

"Really. I've never met anyone who didn't like pizza."

Natalia offered no response, not even a shrug.

"You could bring your own food, or we could add pasta or a sandwich to the order. I've heard everything from Luigi's is wonderful."

"No, thanks." Natalia's gaze flickered to the bicycle. "Is Joe inside?"

"Yes. He's changing clothes." Liz's stomach clenched, and her temperature spiked.

"Tell him I'll replace his pillow. Have fun."

Before she disappeared, Liz spoke again quickly. "Natalia, seriously—"

"Have fun. Seriously."

And for the first time Liz had seen that didn't involve the puppies, Natalia smiled.

They ate on the porch, the two rockers facing each other with a small table in between to hold the pizza boxes and iced tea. Breaking the last bit of crust into two pieces, Joe tossed one to each dog before he closed the empty boxes and set one on top of the other.

"I love pizza," Liz said with a satisfied sigh.

"It's in your blood, huh?" When she glanced at him, brows raised, he lifted one shoulder. "Josh said you were half Italian."

"On my mother's side. I always thought it would be fun to eat my way through Italy."

"Do you cook Italian food?"

Her smile was faint in the growing darkness. "Does macaroni from a box count?"

"No."

"I don't cook." Before he could respond, she raised one finger to make her point. It was slender, the nail curved gently and polished the same shade as her toes. "I can. I just don't."

"I can and I do. Mostly Cuban."

She tilted her head to one side to study him. Did she have a clue how incredibly relaxed and beautiful and sexy she looked? He doubted it. That was okay, though, because he damn well knew.

"Blond hair and blue eyes. You don't fit my stereotyped image of a Cuban."

"My father's not Latino, but his adoptive parents were."

"I didn't know that."

Bear came around to sniff the napkin resting on Joe's leg. He pushed the dog away, then crumpled the napkin into a ball. "Why should you? Josh was never big on heritage or family or much of anything besides himself."

"And yet people love him."

All sense of ease fled as Joe's muscles tightened. Half surprised he could unclench his jaw to speak, he asked sharply, "Do you?"

She drew her gaze to him, her dark eyes rounded. "Love Josh?"

"You were with him a long time." His tone was accusing, but he couldn't soften it. "You must have felt *something*...I don't know...serious? Significant?"

He would bet his next shipment of Salvadoran strictly high-grown Arabica that she wouldn't have answered at all if she could have avoided it. As it was, her answer was a non-answer. "It was...complicated."

His laughter was short and sharp. "With Josh, everything is complicated."

Her own laugh was rueful. "You're not too simple yourself."

"Of course I am. What you see is what you get."

She looked as if the idea of "getting" might tempt her. It had better. If he were the only one wanting things, the only one who'd damn near burst into flames at the simple touch of her fingers around his hand, life truly wasn't fair.

Elizabeth shot to the edge of the porch, nose quivering, and Bear joined her with a shuffle, staring into the deepening shadows with the same intensity. Liz watched them, smiling faintly. "Are you missing a pillow?"

"Yeah. From my bed. The best one I ever had. I figure Elizabeth is responsible. She has this defiant *screw-you* look when she does something wrong. She probably smelled me on it and that's why she shredded it."

"Natalia said she would replace it."

"Nah. I'll ask Mom where she bought it—" Abruptly he broke off. He wouldn't get comfortable enough with Liz to talk about his parents. Not when he couldn't trust her.

But she didn't pounce on his slip, try to get more information out of him or even look at him. She continued to watch the dogs as they stared out a moment longer, then, with Elizabeth in the lead, returned to their places against the wall and curled up. After a long time, she said, "I'm not in love with him."

Relief seeped through him, his muscles easing from tension that had become so familiar he only noticed it when it was gone. He would tell himself it didn't matter whether she loved Josh, but unlike his brother, he wasn't in the habit of lying. It did matter.

For whatever it was worth.

"Then why are you looking for him?" He was surprised at how even his voice was, as if he didn't give a damn about the subject.

"I've told you."

"Yeah, yeah, he's got something you want. What?"

"Charm to spare?"

He scowled at her, even though she still wasn't looking at him. She must have sensed it, though, because she did meet his gaze at last. "I'll make you a deal, Joe. I'll tell you why I'm looking for Josh right after you tell me where your parents are."

He scooted his chair away from the table so he could stretch out his legs. "Ain't ever happenin', darlin'."

She mimicked his drawl. "Ditto, darlin'."

After a moment, he asked, "Do you ever miss Kansas?"

"Not the place so much as what it represents."

Home. Family. Simpler times. At least, that was what Chicago meant to him. Truth was, he hadn't realized how much it meant to him until he had to leave it.

"Are you ever going back there to live?"

"I don't know." She folded her arms across her chest as if chilled. "Probably not, though my mother wonders how I could even consider raising her grandbabies in any other state."

"Planes fly to all fifty of them. You'll visit." But he understood. His parents had chosen to make their new home in Savannah in part because it was only two hours from Copper Lake. She might never see Josh again, his mother had sniffed, but she would always be close enough to spend an afternoon with Joe's kids.

Assuming he found someone to marry and have them with, and no way was Liz that someone.

"Try telling my mother that a visit with her only grandchild is sufficient." She tucked her feet into the seat of the rocker. "Is it different with sons? Does your mother nag you? Has she already got plans for the son or daughter you don't yet have?"

"Of course. She intends to do all the things we did with our grandmothers—teach him to cook, have Saturday night sleepovers, let him get away with breaking all the rules we had to abide by."

"Rules you abided by," Liz pointed out. "Not Josh."

"Yeah." He tilted his head back, letting his eyes close. Besides Bear's snuffles and the steady drip of the rain, distant music drifted. Country, with the dominant whine of a steel guitar. "Nat's got the blues."

The rocker creaked as Liz presumably twisted to see the other house. "I invited her to dinner, but she said no. She's an interesting girl."

"Girl? She's just a few years younger than you."

"But she seems so young."

He knew exactly what she meant. Natalia pretended to be tough, but she was one of the most vulnerable women he'd ever met. The people who should have protected her and made her feel safe had done a lousy job of it, and he felt as if he needed to make up for it but didn't know how other than by being friends with her. He suspected the damage already done was so great that a little thing like friendship couldn't begin to repair it.

"I didn't figure you for the waif type."

It took a moment for Liz's comment to sink in, and when it did, he grinned. He liked Natalia a lot, maybe even sort of loved her in a big-brother-kid-sister way, but when it came to steamy, hot, wicked sex, it wasn't big-eyed vulnerable Nat who turned him on. She didn't even enter the picture, thank you, God. Just the thought struck him as perverse.

"Nat and I are buddies." He emphasized the last word. "My type is…" He glanced at her peripherally: black curls, outfit that was neither particularly snug nor revealing but sexy as hell anyway, killer legs, bare feet, expression guarded— not too open, not too friendly, not too invested. Yeah, right.

He left the sentence hanging as the breeze freshened, and she shivered, rubbing her hands over her arms. He stood, gathered the pizza boxes and glasses, then opened the screen door. Elizabeth and Bear shot past him, rocketing through the living room and into the kitchen. "Want to come in?"

It was a stupid invitation that she had luckily refused the first time. He no more wanted her inside his house, touching his things, leaving her scent on the air, than he'd wanted her in his car with Josh two years ago. If he'd turned down his brother's request, he wouldn't have gotten shot, at least not that day.

Would Josh have been shot instead? And maybe Liz, too, because she was with him? Would either of them have been as lucky as Joe had? Or would one or both of them be dead now?

He touched one wrist to his ribcage, where a scar marked the entrance wound of the second bullet. That was the first time in two years that he'd considered himself lucky.

She hesitated so long that he thought she was going to turn him down again, but then she got up and walked to the door, slipping past him with so little room to spare that he'd swear he felt the air ripple between them.

His house was laid out exactly like hers: living room, eat-in kitchen, bedroom, bath. He hadn't brought any furniture from Chicago. All the leather and chrome stuff had sold with the condo. Instead, he'd borrowed a few pieces from Miss Abigail in the beginning while he looked for what he wanted: old oak and pine for the wood pieces, overstuffed comfort for the upholstered ones. Color brightened the walls, and rugs warmed the wood floors. It was cozy, his mother had proclaimed on her one visit. He preferred to think comfortable.

What did Liz think?

She hardly glanced at the television that dominated one corner of the living room but turned her attention instead to the bookcases. They were filled with books, both fiction and nonfiction, and stacked in one shelf corner was a pile of magazines. He watched stiffly as she picked up the top one, glanced it, then laid it back. He usually recycled magazines as soon as he finished with them, but he'd kept these to camouflage the one at the bottom. Alone, it would rouse interest. Just part of a pile, no one noticed it.

Next she glanced at the wicker basket that stored paper for recycling, then a group of pictures on the wall: his parents on their wedding day, both sets of grandparents and all of his great-grandparents in their youth. Everything more recent—everything including Josh—was packed in a box in the attic.

She stopped in the kitchen door. The dogs had checked their food dishes, upended now in the middle of the floor, then vacated. They were probably on his bed, seeing what other trouble they could cause, but Joe didn't go looking for them. He watched Liz's gaze skim the counters as if nothing there held any interest to her, besides possibly the coffee maker. She scanned the walls, with their photos and framed recipes, handwritten by various long-gone women in his family, and the square oak table that took too much room. "You actually live here," she remarked.

"Did you think I slept in the storeroom at the shop and just changed clothes here?"

"Didn't you pretty much use your condo for just changing clothes?"

He smiled ruefully as he brushed a patch of Bear's fur from the sofa cushions before sitting down. "I didn't like the condo much. Cold and sterile wasn't my idea of home."

"That's what you get for giving an interior decorator free rein." She sat, too, in the armchair, drawing her feet onto the cushions, wriggling into its depths. "The only place to sit in my house is the wicker sofa that belongs on Mrs. Wyndham's porch. It's nice, but I do miss solid furniture."

"I used that sofa, too, when I moved in." Had sat on it, eaten dinner on it, slept on it with his feet hanging over the arm. "But you're not staying long enough to need real furniture."

Her only response was a shrug.

He didn't move—sprawled on the sofa, one arm resting along its back, legs stretched out underneath the coffee table— but the tension ratcheting through him made him feel as if he'd compressed in place. "If I knew where Josh was, I'd tell you."

"To get rid of me?"

To save me. "But I don't know."

"He'll come here."

"He'll go somewhere. He's got a lot of friends and relatives who haven't moved in the last two years. It'll be easier to get help from them than to bother finding me."

"Relatives who know where you are? Where your parents are?"

Joe stared at a painting on the wall, an oil done decades ago by a great-great-grandmother he'd never met. It was one of the few possessions her daughter had been able to bring to the U.S. when she fled Havana. It wasn't very well done, the brush strokes too heavy, the perspective too fuzzy. It was like looking at the city through cloudy glass, but it held sentimental value.

Josh held sentimental value, too. Not necessarily to him, but to some of his friends. Dory's best friend had been appalled when Dory asked everyone not to give Josh any information about them or Joe. *He's your son, your own flesh and blood! How can you turn your back on him?*

Nothing, Opal had declared, could ever make her abandon her children, and she was ashamed that her friend could even think about doing so. If Josh contacted her—not likely but always possible—she might give it a second thought, but in the end, she would give him their addresses and phone numbers.

Maybe a warning phone call to Opal was in order. Maybe Thomas P. Smith, U.S. Attorney's Office, would make it for him.

"What did you guys do after I left Chicago?"

Liz combed her fingers through her hair before resting her cheek on her fist. "Josh figured getting out of town was the safest thing for him, too."

"And you went with him." She didn't love him now, she'd said, but had she then? Giving up her home and her job, if she'd had one, to leave town with a man whom other people wanted dead... That required a serious commitment, didn't it?

She gave no sign of it. "It's not as if Chicago was my home. I'd been there long enough. It was time to go someplace else."

"Where?"

"We moved around a lot. Made it all the way west to San Francisco."

"And *he* left *you*."

"Amazing, isn't it?" Her smile was wry.

It was amazing. On the one hand, Josh had never stayed with one woman that long. On the other…you just didn't walk away from a woman like Liz.

Why would any man with breath in his body want to?

"Why the coffee shop?" she asked while he was still looking for an answer to his own question. "There must have been other small businesses for sale. Were you already a java connoisseur?"

"Nope. I drank my fair share of it, but before I came here, I didn't even own a coffee maker. It just seemed…" Everything about the day he'd made the decision was clear in his memory. He'd been driving, neither knowing nor caring where he was going besides away from Chicago. He'd reached Copper Lake around noon and stopped for lunch at Ellie's Deli. Afterward, he'd walked around downtown to delay climbing back into the car again, and he'd realized that for the first time in six months, he hadn't looked over his shoulder once. It had seemed a sign. Then he'd seen the real sign—*For Sale*—taped in the front window of a shop bearing his name. He'd gone inside and walked out two hours later with an obligation and a new hometown.

"Right," Liz supplied quietly. "It seemed right."

He nodded. "Back then all I knew about coffee was that the good stuff was really good and the bad was really bad, but it beat not having any at all. The first thing I did, besides shutting down the place to remodel, was start researching coffee. *Now* I'm a connoisseur. Back then I was just ready for a new start. Doing what didn't really matter."

She was quiet a long time, her expression wistful. Was she ready for a new start, too? Looking for closure to her two-plus years with Josh so she could move on with her life? And where would she make that new start? Back in Chicago? At home in Kansas?

Copper Lake could always use another waitress, bartender or clerk.

When he could seriously think that thought, it was time for the evening to end. Too much time alone with Liz was a dangerous thing. She needed to go, even if it was just across the yard to the peach house. But before he could fake a yawn or think of an excuse to send her away, claws skittered across the wooden floor, then a crash sounded behind him.

He jumped to his feet, the familiarity of old alarm rushing through him, and spun around, expecting to see the door kicked in or the window glass shattered.

It was nothing so dramatic. The oak-and-brass coat rack beside the door lay on its side, jackets, ball caps and bike helmet scattered around it. Bear was slinking along the wall, heading for safety elsewhere, but Elizabeth stood in the middle of it, one end of her leash still looped over a brass hook, the other in her mouth.

Liz tried to stifle a laugh. "I think she's trying to tell you that it's time for her evening walk."

Joe scowled at her over his shoulder as he circled the couch. "You said you're developing a soft spot for her. Take her, and you can have Bear for free."

As he spoke, Bear weaseled up next to the chair where Liz sat, put one paw up, then wiggled his body into the narrow space beside her. Once he was snuggled against her, with her arm protectively around his shoulders, he gave Joe a mournful look before hiding his face.

Elizabeth, on the other hand, stood in the middle of the floor, still holding the leash and looking defiant.

"You shouldn't say such things in front of your babies," Liz scolded. "See, you've frightened Bear."

Joe reached for the other end of Elizabeth's leash, and she darted off, dragging the six-foot length of webbing behind her.

She caught the end table, knocking it forward a few inches and causing the lamp to sway, then upended the recycling basket on her way into the kitchen. Hands on his hips, he stood where he was, listening to the leash's metal hook clanking behind Elizabeth as she ran in dizzying circles through the house, watching Bear cuddle closer to Liz, his eyes open just enough to give what Joe was pretty sure was a triumphant look, and he sighed.

Hadn't he known he was in trouble the day Liz Dalton walked through the door?

Chapter 6

Taking pity on Joe, Liz pushed Bear to the floor, more difficult than it should have been, given that he was a puppy, then stood up. "Elizabeth," she said sharply. "Want to go for a walk?"

For a moment, the scratch of nails and clanging of hook stilled, then the dog shot into the living room from the hallway, skidding to a stop in front of her and dropping the leash.

"Eww," Liz said, picking it up with two fingers. "There's slobber on the end you have to hold."

"Natalia bought extras. Apparently, the mutt likes to chew on them." Joe set the coat stand back on its clawed feet, returned the coats and hats to their hooks, tossed a blue leash on the sofa, then got another one from down the hall.

Elizabeth was a perfect princess while Liz got her hooked up—an act, she was pretty sure, for Joe's benefit. She wondered if he'd care if she tagged along or if this was her cue to go home. Maybe he'd rather take the walk with Natalia. Maybe he'd rather be alone. A part of her wouldn't mind that.

But the bigger part would rather delay saying good-night to him.

Joe put on a lime-green slicker before attaching Bear's leash and opening the door. Liz accompanied Elizabeth onto the porch, where she slid her feet into her shoes, waiting for an invitation that wasn't likely to come. Finally she said, "Thanks for sharing dinner with me."

"Thanks for providing it." He locked the door, then moved to stand beside them at the top of the steps.

It was still raining, a steady patter that dripped from the roof and ran in miniature rivers across the sidewalk. To be totally comfortable, it needed to be about ten degrees warmer, but lately, being cold had been the least of her worries.

She held out Elizabeth's leash, a smile fixed on her mouth, even when Joe was obviously careful not to touch her when he took it. "I'll see you."

He murmured something, maybe just a sound, and the four of them went down the steps together. Joe and the dogs stopped on the sidewalk while she headed through puddles toward her house. She was halfway there when Elizabeth let out a wail of protest, supported by Bear's barks.

"Hey," Joe called, and Liz turned so quickly that in the rain-unworthy clogs, she was lucky she didn't sprain an ankle. "Why don't you change shoes and go with us? I'll grab another slicker. Okay?"

Wanting to was a bad idea, especially with the way her pulse quickened and her mouth tugged into a goofy grin. *Kick off the shoes and run like hell,* her inner voice advised, but just for a while, she wasn't going to listen. "Okay."

She let herself into the house, moving quickly before he had a chance to retract his invite. In the bedroom, she traded her skirt for shorts, tugged on socks and buckled on her favorite Rocket Dog sneakers, then slung her purse with the .45 over her head and one arm. By the time she'd tucked her cell phone into her pocket and locked the door, Joe and the dogs were waiting on the porch.

She shrugged into the slicker he offered, this one lemon yellow, zipped it up and tried not to be obvious as she inhaled the scent of him from the cotton lining. She didn't recognize his cologne, but it would probably haunt her dreams again tonight.

They crossed the grass to the road, then turned toward the street. Mrs. Wyndham's house was mostly dark, the only lights in an upstairs room. The place looked lonely in the night rain.

"I don't think I could live alone in a house that big," Liz remarked as they reached the end of the driveway and turned onto the sidewalk.

"Me neither. But Miss Abigail's lived here since she got married at nineteen, first in the blue house, then the big one."

"So the cottages weren't servants' quarters."

"No. The old Mrs. Wyndham, Abigail's mother-in-law, had six kids and built the cottages as a way to keep them close. They moved out of her house. They moved into a cottage. The houses were small, originally two bedrooms, no kitchen, because she intended that the children, and their families when they had them, would do most of their living in the main house—meals, entertaining, et cetera."

"She wasn't a little controlling, was she?"

Joe laughed. "Her plan worked for about ten years, until the families began outgrowing the houses. Abigail was pregnant with their third child when the old lady died. Abigail's husband, as the oldest, got the house, and she's lived there ever since."

Liz let Elizabeth drag her off the sidewalk to investigate

something in the shadows of an azalea. "I wouldn't want to live in my mom's backyard as an adult, especially if I were married. But cottages like that would be great when all of us go home for a visit at the same time."

"Are your brothers married?"

"Nope."

"Any kids?"

"Not that I'm aware of." Sam, Max and Eric were good guys. If any of them had a child, they would have taken the responsibility and made the kid a part of the family. If they didn't, their mother, Emilia, would have done it for them. "Which would you prefer? Sons or daughters?" She moved out of the way after Elizabeth had peed on the bush so Bear could do the same, then they continued along the street.

"Boys."

"Girls," she disagreed. "Favorite holiday?"

"What is this? One of those e-mail surveys without the e-mail?"

She laughed. "It's called getting to know you. Come on, favorite holiday. Like every child, elf and adult in the world doesn't know the answer to that one."

In the dim light from the street lamp he scowled at her. "Fourth of July."

"You just said that to be difficult, because the right answer is Christmas."

They reached an intersection, and Bear sniffed the Stop sign while Elizabeth strained hard at her leash and stared intently into the darkness behind them. Aware of the comfortable weight of the pistol beneath her slicker, Liz looked in that direction, too, seeing nothing but rain, trees, shadows and brightly lit houses. Natalia had laughed about Elizabeth going on alert if a butterfly fluttered or a leaf rustled. She hadn't been exaggerating.

"Look at me," Joe said. He hadn't bothered pulling up the hood of his slicker, and his hair was plastered, dark gold, to his head. His jeans were damp and getting damper where Bear's wet leash was wrapped once around his legs—and again around the Stop sign. "I have these dogs, global warming, a slow economy and you hanging around looking for Josh. I don't have to say things to be difficult. My *life* is difficult."

Liz made a dismissive sound. "You're a lucky man, and you know it. You have these two wonderful pets giving you unconditional love, you're doing your best to slow global warming and to help the economy and you've got me hanging around brightening your days. What more could you ask for?"

He stared at her a moment, his mouth twitching before he finally grinned. "Josh is good at twisting things around. Did you learn from him?"

The grin made her warm all the way down to the toes of her soggy shoes, but the mention of Josh chased away all that warmth. She tugged at Elizabeth's leash to get her moving again and stepped off the curb into the street. "Can we have just one conversation that doesn't include your brother?"

They were approaching the other curb by the time Joe untangled himself and Bear and caught up. "Hey, you're the one looking for him."

"For the last couple years, everything's been all about Josh. Can I have a break for one evening?" From the moment she'd been assigned the case, he had been the focus of her life. It was impossible to forget he existed—especially when she saw his face every time she looked at Joe—but she would love to try.

"If you want a break, you could forget about finding him and go back to wherever and do whatever." After a few steps, he asked, "Where would that be? And what would you be doing?"

Where would be Dallas, and *what* would be taking on other

cases. Maybe she could get an easier assignment, like escort-
ing convicted felons to federal prison. But those weren't
answers she could give him.

"Someplace smaller than San Francisco and Chicago.
Doing the usual jobs." She gave him a sidelong look. "Maybe
someplace small enough that I could get a bike and ride to
work. I haven't been on one in twenty years, but they say you
never forget."

"Borrow Natalia's and we'll go for a ride Sunday. You can
see where Copper Lake gets its name."

"Sure, if Natalia doesn't mind. Although I may do good to
not fall off in front of the house."

"You keep your balance in those ridiculous heels. You can
keep your balance on a bike."

"You like those ridiculous heels."

His smile was faint, serious, and his voice husky. "Hell, yeah."

If she'd been wearing heels, she would have been lucky to
reach the curb to sit down before she fell. Her legs were that
weak.

Because she didn't have a clue what to say and he seemed
to have no follow-up, they fell silent for a while. An occasional
car passed, its wipers working to keep the windshield clear.
It was after nine o'clock on a Friday night, and the closer they
got to downtown, the more activity there was—traffic, other
people hurrying their pets through their evening business,
bright lights shining in the few businesses that were still open.

"Football or baseball?"

Liz glanced at Joe.

"Which do you prefer?"

Ah, the survey. "Actually, basketball. The shortest of my
brothers is six-four so they had to play whether they wanted
to or not, and I had to go to the games to support them. I don't
have to ask you. I know it's baseball."

"Hey, it paid my way through three years of college."

"You were that good?"

He shrugged. "Good enough for college ball, not a chance in hell at going pro. I focused on classes the last year, since that was going to earn me a living. Baseball wasn't."

"I'm impressed." Not that she hadn't already been impressed with him.

"Winter or summer?"

They stood at the intersection across from A Cuppa Joe, waiting for cars to pass. Only a few lights were on inside the shop, and she had no doubt they were the funky reduced-energy curly kind. "That depends on whether you mean winter like in Colorado or in Southern California. I don't like cold."

"Me neither." Bear was starting to drag, and Joe gave him an encouraging word. "Paper or plastic?"

Liz laughed. "Like I don't know the right answer to that. I saw those canvas shopping bags on your kitchen table. I'll probably even be tempted to buy a couple of my own next time I'm at the grocery store."

"Watch out. Before you know it, you'll be looking at hybrid cars and local produce and giving up paper towels for real ones."

She laughed again as they strolled to the end of the street, then turned into the square, following the path to the gazebo. Its roof provided a nice respite from the rain, letting her tug down the slicker's hood and shake out her curls. She drew a deep breath of damp, fresh air and faded cologne and knew if she stepped close enough, she could smell the same scent, warm and sexy, on his skin. The thought made her shiver.

Leaning against the railing a few safe feet away, Joe asked, "Are you cold?" His voice was husky again, and she could tell by the way he looked at her that he already knew the answer. How could she be cold when all she had to do was stretch out her hand and touch him? When one step was all it would take to bring her body into contact with his?

"A little," she lied.

"Maybe we should keep moving."

Maybe we should move together. What would he do if she said that aloud? Point out the reasons they shouldn't? Pretend he misunderstood? Or agree?

Her hand was as shaky as her smile when she pulled the hood back into place. "Yeah, I guess we should."

They went down the opposite steps, Elizabeth balking at going back into the rain. Finally she relented, but retaliated as they reached the sidewalk by showering them both with water.

They were walking alongside the iron fence that encircled River's Edge, not talking, the sort of silence shared by two people who were comfortable with each other. She didn't feel the need to talk—just to jump his bones—and he apparently didn't want idle chatter either.

As they neared the side gate, an engine back down the block revved and tires squealed. Liz glanced over her shoulder at the dark SUV barreling down the street. *Kids,* was her first thought. All three of her brothers thought faster was better and, as teenagers, had always believed they had more control over the vehicle than was true.

Then the driver passed the last car parked in the street, jerked the wheel and drove up over the curb with a jarring bounce, heading right for them. Instinctively she reached for her gun, realized it was impossible to access and grabbed Joe's arm instead. Thankful that the gate opened on first shove, she dragged him and the dogs through it, one swearing, the others yelping. They stumbled into the yard, landing in one tangled mass.

Liz hit the ground hard, her bag shifting underneath so that the .45 was in the middle of her back. Pain stabbed through her, hot and sharp, but she shoved herself up enough to catch a last glimpse of the fleeing truck: black, two-door, no tag, two occupants. She sank down again, aware of the throb in her back, the water pooling around her, the leash wrapped around her calves, and silently matched Joe curse for curse.

He jerked free of her and the dogs before rising to his knees and working the leashes loose. His hands on her shoulders as he helped her sit up were gentle in contrast to his voice. "Are you okay?"

She nodded.

"Who the hell— What the hell was that?"

Gingerly she took a slow breath, deepening it until it hurt, before meeting his grim look. "My best guess is that it's a warning."

The question was, from whom?

Joe stood, gripping both leashes in one hand, and offered Liz a hand. He didn't miss her wince as he pulled her to her feet. His movements jerky, he walked a few feet away, cussed, then came back. "A warning from whom? The Mulroney brothers? The feds? Or is someone else involved in this mess that I don't know about?"

She shrugged, wincing again, and he unclenched his fist to touch her arm. Even through the cold vinyl, he could feel her heat, radiating, luring, tempting his fingers to move nearer, underneath the slicker, underneath her shirt to bare skin.

Probably bruised bare skin. "Did you land on something?"

"My purse." Her smile was wry. "It felt like hitting a brick."

"Do you need to go to the hospital? I can call someone."

"No hospital. But maybe it would be better if you could get us a ride."

"I'll call Nat." He moved under the spreading branches of a huge live oak before pulling out his cell phone and calling

Natalia's number. It rang five times before a canned record-ing came on: *This is Natalia. Leave a message.*

Jeez, where was she? She didn't party, didn't go to bars, didn't have a social life outside of him. He was considering his next best choice—Pete Petrovski, who did have a social life—when an SUV pulled to the curb and Tommy Maricci rolled down the passenger window.

"You guys look like drowned rats. Especially that one." He gestured toward Elizabeth, who raised her head regally and bared her teeth.

"Look, Liz," Joe said drily. "We need someone to serve, and public service is in his job description."

Maricci's gaze shifted to Liz, revealing the kind of appre-ciation breathing men probably always showed her, though she was too preoccupied to notice, staring in the direction their would-be hit-and-runners had disappeared. Her lack of notice satisfied Joe in ways he wouldn't consider at the moment.

"Come on. I'll give you a ride. Even the rat and the walking furball."

"Thanks." Joe took a couple steps, then, when Liz didn't move, backtracked and reached for her arm. He stopped, though, not sure where she was hurting, not wanting to cause her pain. "Hey. Come on. Let's get out of the rain."

She blinked, focused her gaze on his hand, still hovering a millimeter from her arm, then blinked again. "Yeah. I think I've had enough for one day."

Neither dog needed any urging to get into the truck; Joe opened the rear door and they leaped inside. Liz eased into the backseat before reaching for the seat belt. He got it first, pulling the strap across her chest, leaning closer to fasten the buckle near her hip. She was pale, her expression unreadable. She murmured, "Thanks," in a toneless voice, then huddled deeper in the slicker.

"What were you doing at River's Edge?" Maricci asked as Joe settled in the passenger seat. "I thought the gates were locked up at night."

"So did I." Good thing that side gate had been open tonight. Getting caught between it and a two-ton vehicle would have been a sorry end to their walk in the rain. "I was looking for a dry place to use my phone."

"The coffee shop's sixty feet away and you choose the questionable shelter of a tree?"

Joe's face felt too frozen to grin, but he managed anyway. "Then we would have made a mess, and I would have to clean it or Esther would bite off my head in the morning. Kind of like the mess the dogs are making back there." To be fair, though, they hadn't given a single shake and seemed content to sit and look out the back window.

"Yeah, you're lucky I'm driving my own vehicle. If I'd had my department car, I would've left you standing. No drunks, no smokers, no food, no animals or people who smell like them in the Charger."

"Is that police policy?"

"That's Maricci policy."

"So what are you doing out on a night like this if you're not working?"

"Waiting for Ellie to get off. A couple of waitresses were no-shows this evening, so she stayed to help out."

"That can't be fun in her condition."

Tommy snorted. "Even in her 'condition,' she could take you and me both."

Joe glanced over his shoulder at Liz, silent and still. Was she uncomfortable with cops? Remembering when he'd said he would turn Josh over to Maricci if he showed up in town? Still shaken by their near-miss?

Joe was still shaken.

He and Maricci talked about nothing the rest of the way home. Maricci pulled into the parking space next to Joe's house, then gave him a wry look. "Pollution, ozone and the environmental impact of drilling for oil aside, there are times when a car comes in handy, man."

"Yeah, but walking the dogs isn't one of them. Thanks for the ride." Joe climbed out, then freed the dogs while Liz slid from the backseat. As Maricci backed out, they walked to the sidewalk that connected the three west-side houses. If he hadn't still been mildly freaked out, he wouldn't have noticed the movement on Natalia's porch, but jumpiness made him look sharply in that direction.

In the dim light spilling from the living room window, Natalia was pulling off her shoes. She wore jeans and a dark slicker, the hood still pulled over her head.

His heart rate slowed a few beats. "Hey, Nat. Can you do me a favor?"

She stiffened, then shoved the hood back from her head. "Joe. I didn't hear…"

That was why he never wore the hood on those things. "Can you take the dogs to my house and start drying them off? Liz fell while we were walking, and I want to get her inside."

"Sure." Ignoring her shoes, she came down the steps bare-footed, took his keys and the dogs and headed next door.

"I can walk fifty feet by myself," Liz commented.

"Yeah, and I can dry those mutts off by myself, but I'd rather not."

In less than a minute, they were standing on her porch, stripping off their slickers, taking off their shoes. Liz pulled her keys from her bag and unlocked the door, and he followed her inside.

Their cottages might be identical in construction and layout, but that was where the similarities ended. His was comfortable—okay, even cozy—while hers was so empty that it echoed. The wicker sofa and matching coffee table were the only things in the living room, and except for a foam cup from SnoCap, the kitchen looked as if it hadn't been used in decades. No pictures on the walls, no rugs on the floor, not a single personal thing anywhere besides the laptop computer on the table.

She went down the hall to the bathroom, then came back with a couple of towels. "Welcome to my humble home."

"That's one way of putting it. Jeez, even rent-by-the-hour motel rooms have more personality than this."

"And you have a lot of experience with rent-by-the-hour motel rooms?"

He scowled at her. "You don't even have a television."

"I don't watch much TV, and I can catch some of my favorite shows online."

"No stereo?"

"I listen to music on the computer or my iPod."

"Books? Newspapers?"

She gestured to the computer.

"Do you at least have a bed?"

She finished drying her feet and legs, then straightened to give him a long, level look. "I do. Want to see it?"

The towel had become unnecessary. The heat rising inside him spread through his veins, warming his skin, turning moisture to steam. He couldn't hear the sizzle, though, over the roaring in his ears. He didn't want to see her bed. He wanted to be in it. With her. For a long, long time. The rest of the weekend sounded like a good start.

He looked around for a place to lay the towel, then wrapped it securely around his fists. "No, thanks," he said, half surprised his voice worked, though it sounded harsh and very much as if he were lying. "But I would like to see where you fell."

She looked for a moment as if she'd forgotten about it, then gave a lopsided shrug. "It's okay."

"Just a look. Turn around."

The look in her eyes suggested she was debating an argument, then, with a frown, she turned her back to him. Her purse came off first, dangling from her fingers to land with a clunk on the wood floor. Next she grasped the hem of her shirt and slowly peeled it up. Halfway to her shoulders, she stopped and stood motionless.

Just beneath the scrunched fabric was the band of her bra, narrow, lacy, black. Damn. Underneath that was skin, smooth, olive-toned, stretching across bone and muscle, tapering in at her waist, starting to flare again before her shorts blocked the view. Not a lot of skin. Not as much as he regularly saw on joggers and swimmers and girls at the shop. But it was Liz's skin, and from the moment he'd met her, he'd wanted to see it, touch it, kiss it.

He closed his eyes briefly, took a shallow breath, then dropped the towel and walked to her. There was a mark in the middle of her back above her waist, where the skin dipped slightly over her spine, red and scraped, promising to add more colors to its palette by morning. He touched it gently and she shivered. Not because her skin was warm and his fingers were cold. He knew that instinctively.

"You'll have a good bruise tomorrow." His voice was thick, strained.

So was hers. "It won't be the first. Three brothers, remember?"

He was warm and getting warmer. His fingers were still on her back, tracing lightly, and she wasn't moving or pushing him away. It would be so easy to put both hands at her waist—*like that*—then to slide them up her arms—*like that*—then grasp her shoulders and turn her to face him.

Like that.

There was a smear of dirt on her cheek where she'd fallen, and her curls looked like coiled springs that were about to explode, but she was gorgeous. Her dark gaze locked with his, her eyes hazy with desire and regret, and he figured he looked about the same. He wanted her, damn it, but there were good reasons for both of them to keep their distance, starting with Josh.

Then she sighed softly, and he thought to hell with Josh. All their lives, Joe had been the responsible, reliable, honorable twin, while Josh had done what he wanted, taken what he wanted and run when he wanted. Joe had always thought too much, and Josh hadn't thought at all.

At this moment, Joe didn't want to think. He wanted to feel. To do.

Liz's breathing was shallow, ragged, then he realized that it was his own echoing in his ears. She was hardly breathing at all, waiting, watching him, wanting…

Wanting him for who he was, or because he looked exactly like his brother?

Later, that would matter. All the reasons this was a bad idea would matter. But not right now.

He raised both hands to her face, cupping his palms to her cheeks, lowering his head until his mouth brushed hers. She responded with a breath, another soft sigh, and knotted her fingers in the waistband of his jeans. She was so slender, so delicate, and yet she'd probably saved his life tonight by yanking him through the River's Edge gate.

He brushed her mouth again, rewarded with another whisper of sound from her, then drew back to stare at her. "It'll take more than a mention of Josh to stop me this time."

She stared back as she moved closer, taking the two steps needed to bring their bodies together. His hands moved of their own accord, sliding around to her back, holding her exactly where he wanted her to be.

Rising onto her toes, she murmured into his ear, "That mention of Josh wasn't to stop you. It was to stop *me*."

Remember Josh, she'd said in a panic-tinged whisper. He liked thinking he could have made her forget.

He didn't tease her, play or rush. He just kissed her, all mouths and tongues and tastes and heat and need and hunger and two years' worth of wanting. His heart was pounding, his lungs burning, and all he could think was she was worth the wait.

She was clinging to him when he stopped, or maybe he was clinging to her. He didn't want to let go, didn't want to step back and start thinking. He just wanted to kiss her again and see where it would lead. To bed, for sure. To trouble, absolutely. To disaster—long-time unhappy, hurts to be with her or without her—pretty damn likely.

He touched her hair, stretching out one thick curl, soft and shiny as it reshaped around his fingers. He toyed with it a moment, sighed heavily and rested his forehead against hers. "I'd better go."

Her grip on him tightened, then slowly released. She didn't take a step away, though. She left that to him, and it was damn hard.

"If you want an ice pack for your back…" He'd send Natalia over with it. Once he walked out that door, he couldn't come back, not tonight.

"Thanks, but I've got a half-frozen bottle of water if I need it." Her smile was awkward and not very convincing. "There's a cold spot in the refrigerator where stuff freezes."

"You can't put a water bottle on—" He shook his head. "Never mind. I'll see you."

She let him get to the door before speaking. "Why didn't you tell Detective Maricci what happened tonight?"

With half the room between them, it was safe to face her again. "I didn't see the driver. I can't give a description of the truck that's worth anything. I didn't get the tag number. Did you?"

She shook her head.

"If I'd told him, he couldn't have found the guy, but he still would have wanted to know why I was someone's target. It just seemed pointless." He opened the door, then looked at her again. "Why didn't you tell him?"

She shrugged. "It wasn't my story to tell."

He acknowledged that with a nod. "If you need anything…"

Her smile was unexpected and bright and made him regret that half the room separated them. "I'll call you. And if you need anything…"

After studying her a moment, he reluctantly grinned. "Yeah. Same thing."

Not that he would be calling anyone, he thought as he grabbed his shoes and the slickers, then dashed across the yard to his house. But if he did, she would be the one.

Because she was the only thing he might need.

Chapter 7

When Liz was home in Dallas, Saturdays were usually reserved for sleeping in late, then running errands that she couldn't fit into her lunch hour or after work on week nights. This morning, she'd done the sleeping in, a hard, dreamless sleep, broken only by faint pain when she'd rolled over. Now she lay on her side, staring out the window at a blue sky with fat clouds. She didn't want to get up, didn't want to think, just wanted to lie there and remember.

The touch of Joe's fingers on her back.

The taste of him on her tongue.

The sound of his breathing, ragged in her ear.

The need to kiss him again.

And to never kiss him again.

Her cell phone beeped, and she picked it up from the floor, then shut off the alarm. The marshal Mika was sending from Atlanta would be at the coffee shop by eleven, and she wanted to get there first. Liz shoved back the covers, then planted her feet on the floor. Her back was sore, and she was stiff from such a long, solid sleep, but she gritted her teeth and pushed to her feet.

"You're getting too old for this, Lizzie," she muttered, using her mother's nickname for her and echoing Emilia's sentiments. "Women your age should be married and having babies, not chasing around bad guys."

I've got time, she always answered Emilia.

Maybe you do, but I don't, her mother always retorted. *I want grandbabies while I'm still able to play with them.* As if she weren't in such good shape that she could outlast her husband and all her kids at everything.

Liz did want children. She'd always imagined herself, well-invested in her career, in a supervisory position that would allow her a more regular work schedule and going home to her husband and at least two kids most nights. The husband had always been faceless, but the kids hadn't: one dark-haired, dark-eyed devilish little boy and the other a dark-haired, dark-eyed princess, though without her mother's curls, thank you very much.

But as she stepped into the shower under the rush of hot water and closed her eyes, the kids in the picture that formed were between dark and fair, and their eyes were blue blue blue. Like Joe's.

Damn.

By the time the hot water ran out, her body was more relaxed, even if her emotions were still tied in knots. She dressed in capris and a sleeveless top with sandals, added makeup, earrings and perfume, slung her purse over her shoulder and headed out the door.

Natalia sat on the steps of her house, watching the dogs at play. Bear glanced Liz's way, but Elizabeth was too intent on stalking a butterfly to pay her any attention, and he was reluctant to leave the other dog's side.

"Good morning," Liz called.

"Morning." Natalia drew her knees a little closer and wrapped her arms around them. "How do you feel?"

The question surprised Liz. When she'd called Mika the night before to report the incident, Mika hadn't asked *Are you all right?* or *Was anyone hurt?* She'd gone straight to, *Did you get a description?* "I'm fine. Just a little bruised." Liz slid on her sunglasses, then impulsively said, "I'm going downtown. Would you like to join me?"

For an instant, Natalia looked tempted, then she shook her head. "I hate to keep the puppies locked up too long."

Liz looked at the dogs, who had given up on the butterfly and stretched out in a patch of sunlight that had dried the sidewalk from yesterday's rain. Their eyes were closed, and Elizabeth's head rested on Bear's hip. "I imagine they can sleep inside the house as well as they can outside."

Another instant of hesitation was followed by another headshake. "I don't think so."

With a little more coaxing, Liz thought, she might change her mind. But maybe not. Maybe Liz was the only weak one around.

"I'll see you later, then." She turned, heading for her car, but when she reached it, she didn't open the door. It wasn't far downtown, and it was a beautiful day. Her sandals were comfortable enough for walking, and she wouldn't be contributing to the emissions that dirtied the air.

That last thought caught her off guard. *Watch out,* Joe had said. *Before you know it, you'll be giving up paper towels for real ones.* Not likely. But an occasional walk instead of driving…why not?

It was a pleasant walk. People working in their yards spoke to her, and she spoke back. In between, though, her thoughts remained on the phone call last night with Mika. *Do you think they meant to kill Joe?*

Liz's gut instincts said no. With the weight of the vehicle and the speed at which it was traveling, the decorative iron fence at River's Edge would have collapsed like toothpicks. The driver could have run them down without delaying his getaway by more than a few seconds. If he preferred to avoid damage to the truck, his passenger could have shot them both and, again, they could have disappeared within seconds.

Which meant it was either a warning or a random occurrence. Mika didn't like randomness; it didn't fit neatly into her structured view of the world. But the near-miss could have been nothing more than a prank, as Liz had first thought. Kids with more booze than sense. God knew, the world was full of irresponsible people causing unintended consequences.

And you haven't seen anyone you know around town, Mika had confirmed. *Any likely suspects?*

Liz had a passing familiarity with pretty much everyone who worked for the Mulroneys. There might be newcomers other than herself in Copper Lake, but no one she knew from Chicago. Granted, the Mulroneys could have easily hired someone from Atlanta or Augusta or anyplace else. Long-distance hiring for bad guys, especially with the Internet, was no more difficult than for anyone else.

Before she realized it, she was standing across the street from the coffee shop. About half the tables inside were occupied, and the line at the counter hid Joe from sight. Was it better to face him for the first time since that kiss with an audience or alone?

Depended on what she wanted the outcome to be.

Esther was still working, though it was nearly ten-thirty. Her orange hair clashed badly with her pink T-shirt, but she seemed unaware as she greeted Liz with a broad smile and a wink. "Mornin'. I hear you've become quite a regular with Joe, and not just at the shop either. Burgers at SnoCap, pizza at his place, long walks in the rain…"

Small towns and their gossip. "Let me guess. Your granddaughter hangs out at SnoCap, and the pizza delivery guy is an old boyfriend of yours." After all, he couldn't have been more than twenty years old.

Esther laughed heartily. "My granddaughter does hang out at SnoCap—so did I fifty years ago—and the pizza delivery guys are all old students of mine. And I'm keeping my daughter's yappy poodle while she's out of town, and the creature has to go outside every hour on the hour. Do you know I actually have to hold an umbrella over her when it rains?"

"Have you considered diapers?" Liz asked drily as she joined the line.

"Yeah, but I'm too old to be changing 'em and too young to be wearing 'em." Esther laughed again, nudged her with an elbow, then went to top off coffee cups.

In Dallas, none of Liz's neighbors knew her well enough to bother with her comings and goings. As for all the places she'd stayed in the past two years, they'd deliberately kept a very low profile. No one had known anything about them, and apparently hadn't cared. There'd been little curiosity, no neighborly visits, no friendly invitations.

She would appreciate the lack of anonymity in Copper Lake if she didn't have things to hide.

Finally it was her turn to order. The teenager in front of her took his change and frozen drink and Joe's gaze met hers and her lungs tightened. Sure, it was lack of oxygen that made her a little giddy, nothing more.

For a moment, he just looked at her, all serious and hard to read. Then he smiled, just a bit, just a quirk of his mouth, and said, "Hey."

"Hi." She watched him for a moment before remembering that she was supposed to order something. "I'll have a—a—" Her gaze swept over the menu board, but the words didn't make a lot of sense. "Surprise me."

His smile grew a bit. "Hot or cold?"

"Hot."

"Have a seat. I'll bring it out in a minute."

Her head bobbed several times before her feeble brain got her feet moving. She found a table next to the east-facing window, still lit by a sliver of sun. The seat was warm and felt good against her back.

At the counter, Joe was talking with the next customer in line, his voice a quiet rumble. A man's voice was a comfortable thing. Her earliest memories were of awakening at night to the soft murmur of her parents talking in their room next to hers. The conversations were mundane—what he had done at work that day, which cases she was hearing, what kind of trouble the boys had gotten into—but the words hadn't mattered. Just the sound of her father's voice had made her feel safe and secure enough to sleep again.

Joe's voice made her feel safe and secure…and a whole lot more.

Forcing her thoughts from that direction, she looked around the room. The music playing in the background was symphonic, lots of strings and horns. She would have preferred something by Metallica or Nickelback, but the other customers didn't seem to mind. Most of them were plugged into iPods or immersed in conversation. One woman read a book while sipping her coffee. Another typed furiously on her laptop, and the earbud customers were making use of the wireless Internet connection. With the ceiling fans circulating the mixed scents of great brews, it was a lovely way to pass the time.

If she were merely there to pass the time.

Minutes went by before Joe finished with the rest of his customers, then came to the table, carrying a tall glass mug that he set in front of her before sliding into a chair. She didn't ask what it was, but reached for it, blew a small crater in the whipped cream mounded on top, then took a cautious sip. "Oh, my God, this is wonderful. I love hazelnut."

He looked the way a good cook did when presenting a meal done to perfection. "Jamaica Blue Mountain coffee and cream whipped with a little hazelnut infusion."

"This would be incredible on a cold snowy night."

"You don't like cold."

"No, but this would make it tolerable." She took another drink. "Busy morning?"

"About typical. It'll slow down at lunch, then pick up again around two." He glanced around the room before focusing on her again. "How is your back?"

"Bruised." She'd managed a look in the bathroom mirror after her shower and seen muddied colors and slight swelling. At least it wasn't shaped like her pistol. That would have been hard to explain.

"By the time I got home last night, Nat had dried the dogs and they were curled up in my bed. Do you know it's virtually impossible to dry a dog a hundred percent with a towel? I rolled over around two this morning onto a wet spot roughly the size of the two mutts combined and cold as ice. I had to strip the bed and leave the mattress to air dry and spend the rest of the night on the sofa."

Ignore that. Change the subject. Take your coffee and run. But the only thing she ignored was the wise voice in her head. "Hey, I offered to show you my bed."

His voice turned a shade huskier. "If you'd offered again around two, I would have taken you up on it, and we'd still be there. Then Esther would have been on her own this morning, and she'd be serving everyone plain black coffee, no matter what they ordered. She doesn't think much of froufrou drinks."

Liz smiled faintly at the old-fashioned phrase in his deep, quiet voice, though she could imagine it quite well in Esther's gravelly tones.

Suddenly serious, he rested his arms on the table, leaning closer. "Does it matter—Josh and me being twins? Is that why…?"

Liz was slow to understand what he meant, then, as she took a drink of the slowly cooling coffee, it hit her and she almost choked. He thought she'd let him kiss her, that she'd held on so tightly to him, because he looked like his brother? Because she was looking for a substitute for Josh, and who better than his identical twin? "No," she said bluntly. "If it mattered, it wouldn't be in a good way."

He opened his mouth to respond, but before he got the first word out, a man stopped beside their table, waiting for their attention. Like Joe, she glanced his way, automatically cataloging him: male, mid-thirties to early-forties, five foot ten, one-seventy-five, brown hair, brown eyes, forgettable. She had never met him before, but in his line of work—her line—forgettable was a good thing.

His gaze was fixed on Joe, as if she weren't worthy of attention. "Saldana?"

Joe nodded.

"Which one are you? Josh or Joe?"

Hostility radiated from Joe even as he shifted to lean back in the chair, looking every bit as casual and relaxed as Liz knew he wasn't. "Joe. Who are you?"

"You wouldn't happen to have ID to prove that?"

"Yeah. Scars from two bullet holes. Want to see?"

The marshal's gaze flickered down to the general area of the scars. Liz hadn't seen the wounds; they'd been covered with dressings and tape during her one hospital visit. That had been enough to give her a bad dream or two.

"I'd settle for a driver's license."

Joe made a pretense of checking his pockets. "Damn, I must have left it at home again."

"That's convenient. Driving without a license is illegal."

"Don't need one for a bike. Who *are* you?"

"Paul Ashe." In a practiced move, Ashe produced his credentials case from an inside coat pocket. "Deputy U.S. Marshal. I'd like to ask you a few questions."

"Everyone wants to ask a few questions. Let me save you the trouble. No, I haven't seen my brother, I haven't heard from him and I don't know where he is. Would you like a cup of coffee before you go back to Atlanta or wherever the hell you came from?"

Ashe's smile was benign. "I don't drink coffee. It makes me edgy."

Joe's smile matched, but with a sharp bite of anger. "I don't need coffee to make me edgy."

Sitting quietly, sipping her drink, Liz hoped she looked as if she wished she weren't there—and, in some ways, she did. But what she was really wishing was that none of this was necessary. Why couldn't Josh behave like an adult once in his lousy life instead of putting his family through this—questioned like suspects and kept under surveillance. Even if they weren't aware of it.

"When was the last time you talked to Josh?" Ashe asked.

"About two minutes before some guy walked up to me with a gun and pulled the trigger." Joe crossed his arms over his chest. "Last time I'm saying it—I haven't seen him. I haven't talked to him. I don't know where he is."

Liz's fingers tightened around the mug handle. *I haven't talked to him.* A moment earlier, he'd said he hadn't heard from him. Hearing from someone didn't necessarily involve talking. An e-mail, a text message, a letter, a message passed through a friend, a posting on a Web site—there were a lot of ways to communicate without actually talking, and some of them were virtually impossible for anyone else to discover.

Careless phrasing on Joe's part? Or a subconscious slip?

She set the mug on the table, and the sturdy base clunked, drawing Ashe's gaze to her for the first time. He feigned surprise well. "You're Elizabeth Dalton. Last time anyone saw you, you were helping Josh get out of town. Now you show up here with his brother, and we're supposed to believe he's not here, too?"

"I'm also looking for him," she said stiffly. "I haven't seen him in a couple months. I woke up one morning, and he was gone, along with everything we had worth taking."

Skepticism colored Ashe's expression and his voice. "Yeah, right. He just ran out on you."

She met his gaze then. "That's what Josh does. He runs out on people."

"Or maybe he goes someplace, pretends to be his brother, settles in, then sends for his girlfriend. They say the best place to hide is in plain sight. The Mulroneys know now that Josh has a twin. Next time—and there's always a next time—they'll want to be real sure they've got the right brother."

Heat rose in Joe, spreading through his veins with each increasing beat of his heart, tightening his jaw until his teeth ached. Shoving one hand into his hip pocket, he pulled out the battered leather wallet his grandmother had given him when he turned sixteen, jerked out his driver's license and slapped it on the table.

"You said you left your license at home," Ashe said accusingly.

"Yeah, well, arrest me for lying."

The marshal picked up the license, studying it longer than necessary, obviously still not convinced. Why should he be? When they'd still lived at home, Josh had "borrowed" Joe's license on more than one occasion, and no one had ever known. After all, his face matched the picture.

"What do you want? Fingerprints?" Joe reclaimed the license and put it away.

"You're identical twins."

"That means identical DNA. Not fingerprints."

Ashe stared at him a moment before turning his attention to Liz. "So what happened between you two? Did he find someone else? Did you nag at him too much? What made him leave?"

As Joe had thought the night before, Liz definitely wasn't comfortable around cops, but only someone who'd spent too much time watching her would see it. She straightened her shoulders under Ashe's gaze, lifted her chin and evenly replied, "The *why* is none of your business, Mr. Ashe. He left. That's all you need to know."

"Had he been in touch with anyone from home? His family? Old friends? Maybe—" he shrugged "—the Mulroneys? Maybe they offered him big bucks to disappear. Ol' Josh always liked money, didn't he?"

You can never have too much money or too many women, Josh had boasted. Joe had known how he'd gotten the women—that had never been a problem for either of them— but he'd never wanted to know where Josh's money came from. He'd alluded to investments, but there was a world of difference between his brother's idea of investments and his own.

When Liz didn't respond, Ashe turned back to Joe. "How much do you think they'd have to give him to overlook the fact they almost killed you? How much is your life worth to your brother?"

Not a whole hell of a lot. That knowledge hurt somewhere deep inside, but Joe stubbornly ignored it.

New customers came in, but he made no effort to leave the table. Despite his joke about Esther, she was perfectly capable of running things behind the counter without his help.

"They might have offered him money to disappear," Ashe said quietly. "But odds are, they'd rather kill him than pay up. If you know anything, if it's not too late…"

The words were directed to Liz, but hit Joe. That magazine on the shelf at home… Presuming the information was even still good, what would happen if he just turned it over to Marshal Ashe? If they found Josh, they couldn't force him to testify. Sure, they could drag his ass into court, but if he didn't want to cooperate, he wouldn't. Maybe the promise of immunity, if they hadn't already offered it, or the threat of withdrawal, if they had, would open his mouth, but Joe wouldn't bet on it.

No, Josh wouldn't voluntarily testify against the Mulroneys. Whether he had to get by on what he'd taken from Liz or was expecting a nice payoff from the Mulroneys, he'd left San Francisco with every intention of staying away from Chicago.

What if it was already too late? What if Josh was dead, had been dead for the last couple of months? Would Joe know? Twins were supposed to share some sort of intuition, some mental or emotional or genetic connection that couldn't be severed by time or distance. But beyond sharing the same face and DNA, he and Josh had never been particularly close. The odds of his knowing when Josh was in trouble were pretty slim, particularly when he'd been in some sort of trouble his whole damn life.

"If I knew where he was," Liz said, "I wouldn't be here with his brother, would I?"

Ashe looked at Liz a long time, and so did Joe. Her comment hurt a little deep inside, too, but if she realized it, it didn't show. Her forehead was wrinkled in a frown, her mouth set in a thin line.

Finally, Ashe tossed two business cards on the table. "Think about it. Decide if you want to save Josh's neck—if he's alive to save—and give me a call."

Joe pocketed the card without looking at it. "Why weren't you watching him all this time he's been gone?"

"We were. In St. Louis, Kansas City, Denver, Albuquerque, Reno, San Francisco. He managed to give us the slip." Ashe looked chagrined as he said the last words. "We're going to find him again."

"Good luck with that."

As Ashe walked away, Liz picked up the card and tapped it on the table, her movements edgy.

"Did you know they were watching you?"

She shook her head.

"That's freaky, even if you don't have anything to hide, to think that someone is out there, tracking your every move." The *tap-tap* came faster until he pulled the card from her grip. "Hey, you want some lunch? There's a place down the street with the best steaks in town."

"What about Esther? Shouldn't she be off by now?"

"She offered to stay through lunch the minute she saw you waiting to cross the street." He stood, took her mug to the counter and spoke to Esther, then returned as Liz slowly pushed out of her seat. She appeared a bit shaken. By being on the wrong side of an interrogation? It was no fun no matter how innocent you were. Or by the possibility that Josh might be dead, that she might never reclaim whatever he took?

Or by the chance that she might never see him again?

They left the shop and walked half a block before she

spoke. "I don't think Josh got paid off. I don't think he had contact with anyone in Chicago. I would have known."

His chuckle was dry and bitter. "Honey, he could be whispering sweet nothings in your ear and stealing a necklace from around your neck, and you'd never notice it slipping away. Besides, he could have gotten in touch with them after he left."

"I guess." A few more steps, then, "Do you think he's dead?"

"I don't know. I hope not." He felt her gaze on him and shrugged without meeting it. "Look, Josh and I have never been best buds and never will be. But I've never wished him dead. Well, not since we were kids." Although some part of him wished Josh had never existed or, at least, had never known Liz. Then Joe wouldn't feel guilty for wanting her. He wouldn't keep remembering that she'd been Josh's first. He wouldn't wonder whether she preferred Josh to him.

Although if Josh had never been born, the odds that Joe and Liz ever would have met were slim, unless he believed in fate, and he wasn't sure he did.

A Cut Above was located in the middle of the block, in an old brick building that still resembled the butcher shop it had once been. That was just in the front, though, where glass cases were filled with choice cuts of meat for home cooking. Swinging doors led to the restaurant, with hardwood floors, exposed brick walls and lights everywhere to make up for the lack of windows.

The hostess, one of Joe's regulars, greeted him with a smile that doubled in size when she saw Liz, and she led them to a table far from the other diners. "We'll give you a little privacy," she said with a pat on his hand, then another for Liz before leaving them alone.

"We're in clear view of everyone else," Liz pointed out as she took a seat. "How private is that?"

"At least they can't eavesdrop."

"Would they?"

"In a heartbeat."

"Esther's keeping tabs on us," she admitted.

"And she's not the only one. You stick around much longer, who knows what they'll think?"

Smiling uneasily, she opened the menu. He didn't bother with his; he always got the same thing for lunch there.

When she laid down the menu again, the waitress came back. He ordered a rib eye, rare, with all the trimmings; Liz asked for a steak sandwich and sweet potato chips. Alone again, he couldn't think of anything to say, and it seemed Liz couldn't either. She sat there, idly toying with the silverware in front of her.

Correction: He could think of something to say. He just wasn't sure he wanted to say it or hear her response now. But even unpleasant conversation would be better than this awkwardness between them.

"So…"

She looked up.

"If you knew where Josh was, you wouldn't be wasting time here with me."

Her cheeks turned pink, but her gaze didn't waver. "I didn't say I was wasting time."

"Yeah, but…" It had been pretty clear: She was in Copper Lake because she didn't know where else to go, and with Joe because he was her only hope of finding Josh.

What if he gave the magazine to *her?* Would his brother be pissed? Or had he regretted running out on her, but just didn't know how to find her since she'd left San Francisco, too?

Could he be responsible for putting her and Josh together again?

Maybe sometime. But not yet.

"I told you before, I'm not in love with Josh. I never was."

"You sure fooled me. And him."

Unexpectedly she smiled. "Fooling Josh isn't hard. He expects everyone to adore him."

Even though her description nailed his brother, he didn't smile back. "If you didn't love him, why did you go with him when he ran off? Why did you stick around all that time?"

"I don't know. I guess the danger. The excitement. I'd never been with a guy that people wanted dead, unless you count the guys I dated in high school. My brothers were always threatening them. It was a big change from life in Kansas. By the time the excitement faded, staying with him was just habit."

"And if you find him, if he wants you to stay a while longer..."

"I'm not interested. Neither is he." She shrugged. "He's got my cell phone number. You notice he hasn't used it."

The knot in Joe's gut loosened, and for the first time since Marshal Ashe had walked through the coffee shop door, he felt some ease and, along with it, hunger. The sight of the waitress approaching with his salad made his stomach growl.

The woman set a glass of sweet tea in front of Joe and served diet pop to Liz, then presented his salad and a loaf of hot bread with a flourish. "The rest will be out as soon as you're done with that. So...Liz, is it? Nice name. Short for Elizabeth?"

Liz nodded.

"Joe and Liz. Has a good sound to it, doesn't it? Both short and sweet...but not too sweet." She gave Joe a sly smile before strolling away.

Liz rolled her eyes. "Are folks like this with every single adult in town, or are you considered particularly needy?"

"Both. They think it's unnatural that I haven't dated since I moved here."

"Why haven't you?"

He speared a grape tomato covered with blue cheese dressing and chewed it while he considered his answer. People had commented on his single status; they'd tried to fix him up with sisters, daughters, nieces, friends. But no one ever asked him why he always said no.

"Things are different," he said at last. "I used to see a fair number of women, and I liked most of them, but it never really meant anything. I guess I'm waiting for someone..." *Who means something.* Someone who could change his life. Someone who could break his heart.

Liz buttered a slice of bread, then set it, untasted, on the plate. "My dad used to tell the boys that you can't win if you don't play the game."

"Maybe that's part of the problem. It's not a game anymore."

"But how do you know one of the women in town isn't exactly what you're looking for unless you give yourself a chance to find out?"

"I know." It sounded stubborn and more than a little sappy. He didn't believe in love at first sight, but he did believe in chemistry. Attraction.

Like the punch to the gut he'd gotten when he met Liz.

Before he could make himself sound any more emotionally moronic than he already had, the waitress delivered their meal, and the next few minutes were spent eating, *mmm*-ing and generally giving the food the attention it deserved.

"I'm not a clingy woman," Liz remarked halfway through the meal. "I know when to let go. If I didn't *need* to find Josh, I wouldn't have given him a second thought. He didn't break my heart, and I'm not looking for someone to take his place. I'm certainly not looking for someone who reminds me of him as much as you do."

Joe nodded, but didn't say anything.

"We both have reasons why we should keep our distance from each other." She picked up a sweet potato chip and concentrated as if dipping it into the ranch dressing was the most important thing on her mind. "After last night, I don't think those reasons are going to be enough."

He agreed. He shouldn't have kissed her. He'd known that when he did it. But damned if he wouldn't do it again given the chance.

And again.

"You could leave town," he pointed out, even though the words made his fingers tighten on his fork.

"Or you could tell me where Josh is."

"I don't know." He didn't parrot the rest of his usual response—*haven't seen him, haven't heard from him.* He didn't want to lie to her, not again, until he had no other choice.

"Then I can't leave."

"Is it money? Is that what he took? Because if you need money, I have some. You can consider it my last favor to Josh."

She shook her head, then finally dropped the chip, soggy now from its time in the dressing.

"What then? Jewelry? A family heirloom? Some sort of keepsake?" He pushed his plate away so he could rest his arms on the table. "If he stole anything of value, Liz, it's gone. He sold it or pawned it, and finding him won't change that. You'll never get it back."

Once more she shook her head.

Now he was bewildered. "What else could be so important? You said it's not a child."

"Absolutely not." Her vehemence was just right to feel real.

"Does he have some sort of evidence against you? Proof that you did…something?" The image of Liz committing a crime, even something minor, refused to form. Josh was the criminal here, not her. She was a good person, friendly to

Natalia, who didn't make friendliness easy for most people, and kind to the dogs. She liked people, and they liked her. She was honest and real.

And so was Josh, when he wanted to be.

She'd liked the excitement of dating the bad boy. She'd known what he was and she'd stuck around anyway, for more than two years. What exactly did that say about her character?

If Josh could fool people into trusting him, so could she. She'd had a long time to learn the art of manipulation from a master.

But Joe didn't want to believe it. Not when he wanted to have wickedly good sex with her.

"No evidence," she said without even a hint of offense. "I don't share Josh's disdain for the law. The worst thing I've ever done is speed, and I like to jaywalk from time to time."

"So now I know what it isn't." If he believed her, and for whatever reasons—trust, lust—he did. "Are you ever going to tell me what it is?"

"Someday." But she replied with such a wistful note that this time he was pretty sure he couldn't believe her.

After lunch, Joe returned to the coffee shop, and Liz headed home. She should call Mika as soon as she got there and rely on her to smack some sense into her. Being chastised by Mika was always a sobering experience.

As she approached the cottages, she pulled out her cell phone, but when she saw Natalia cautiously backing out of Joe's house, she put it back in her pocket. All that rain the day before, but the grass was dry as she crossed it. "Hi."

Natalia startled and closed the door the last few inches with a thud. From the other side came Bear's frantic barks and Elizabeth's most piercing wail. Glancing over her shoulder, she locked the door, then came to the top of the steps. "If you're not careful, Elizabeth will escape, and Bear goes with her."

"You're a good friend to take care of the dogs like this."

Natalia's eyes, magnified behind rectangular-shaped glasses, were blank for a moment, as if she didn't quite grasp the meaning of the words, then she flushed. "I brought them here."

"What else could you do? They needed a home."

Natalia nodded as she came slowly down the steps. When she reached the bottom, Liz would bet, she was going to bolt for home. Grabbing at the only excuse she could come up with, she quickly said, "Hey, Joe suggested that you might be willing to loan me your bike for a ride tomorrow." She gestured toward the bright green bike on the next porch. "It looks expensive. If you don't want to, that's fine. I'd hate to break it or something."

Natalia's smile was rusty. "It's pretty sturdy. Other than flattening a tire, I don't think you can do anything to it."

"I haven't ridden since I was a kid."

"Until I moved here, I'd never been on a bike. If I can learn at this age, you can remember at your age."

Liz grinned. "Be careful of the way you say 'your age.' After I passed thirty, I got more sensitive about it."

"You're not much older than I am."

When Natalia started toward her house, Liz fell into step with her. "There's a quote from a movie probably made before you were born, something about it not being the years but the mileage."

"*Indiana Jones.* I like movies."

"Me, too. Sitting in a darkened theater, munching on salty, buttery popcorn, guzzling pop because the salt makes me thirsty and hoping I can hold off on going to the bathroom until the end."

Natalia's expression was blank, as if Liz was describing

something alien to her. "I watch them here." She gestured toward her house. The front door was open, and through the screen door filtered what sounded like an intergalactic battle.

"Do you mind if I come in and see your collection?"

Natalia hesitated long enough that a polite person would have rescinded the request, but Liz just smiled and waited. Finally, with a shrug, Natalia climbed the steps, opened the screen door and waited for Liz to enter first.

Like her house, like Joe's, Natalia's door opened into the living room, which wasn't barren, as Liz's was, or cozy, as Joe's was. The furniture—sofa, chair, coffee and end tables— wasn't antique but merely old and heavily worn. The television, muted now, was top quality, and the movies…

Liz's brows arched. There were hundreds of them filling shelves that lined the walls: chick flicks, gangster movies, science fiction, thrillers, comedies, horror and entire seasons of enough TV shows to keep a television station in business for years. Liz circled the room, occasionally pulling out a case, then replacing it.

The information in her files on Natalia was minimal: born and raised in Florida, she'd been an honor student before she dropped out of high school and dropped off the radar. She'd had no driver's license or tax returns in the years since. No arrests either.

Where had she spent that time? Doing what? With a pretty young girl, prostitution was always a possibility. Hardships were a given. But it was a fair bet that an honor student who'd quit school and run away from home was already familiar with hardships of one sort or another. Mrs. Wyndham had thought Natalia had been thrown away, like the puppies, and Liz's instincts agreed.

Aware of Natalia standing motionless, watching her, she turned and smiled. "Wow. Did you buy out a rental store? This makes my little collection at home look pitiful."

"Where is home?"

Liz would have bitten back the word if she could. Instead, she shrugged and perched on the sofa arm. "I don't really have one right now. My parents are storing my stuff for me back in Kansas until I settle down somewhere. Where is home for you?"

Her movements economical, Natalia indicated the room around them. "This is it."

"I mean, where are you from?"

"Everywhere." Natalia sat in the armchair, feet flat on the floor, spine straight. "How is Joe?"

"You tell me." When the blank look appeared, Liz went on. "I don't know him that well." *Lie.* In terms of actual contact, maybe they were still fairly new to each other, but in terms of intensity of contact…she knew him in her bones.

Natalia was silent a long time. "He's a good guy," she said at last.

"And you know that based on past experience with good guys?"

She snorted. "Just the opposite. You put a bunch of nice guys together and hide a loser among them, and I can find him blindfolded."

As Liz slid to sit on the sofa cushion, she suspected that Natalia's loser stories could put her own to shame. Some part of her wanted to know what the girl had been through and how she could help, but another part didn't want to know at all. Sad stories were particularly sad when she knew the person involved.

"It must feel funny, going from his brother to him."

As she considered the comment, Liz's gaze skimmed across the framed art on the wall. Movie posters, of course, mostly for golden-age classics. If she'd truly been Josh's girl-friend, it probably would feel strange. But she hadn't been. "They don't have much in common."

"No family resemblance?"

"Well…" Had Joe told Natalia they were twins? "Yeah, I guess you could say that. But they're very different."

"So Joe's the good brother, and Josh is the loser?"

"Yeah, you could say that, too."

Natalia's features darkened, and her lavender eyes radiated hostility, but just for a moment, the time it took for her to replace the mask. Did that home life she'd run away from— or been kicked out of—include a sister she couldn't live up to? Had she been her parents' bad daughter, their loser?

Liz wished she could magically undo the hurts Natalia had suffered, but she was short on magic. If she had any, she'd fix everyone's problems. She would zap Josh back into custody, conjure a conviction for the Mulroneys and twinkle up a chance for her and Joe. Just a fair chance, with no baggage, no lies, no Josh between them. That was all she would ask for.

As if she'd had all the conversation she could stand, Natalia got to her feet. "Do you want to give the bike a ride now so you'll be ready tomorrow?"

"So I can dazzle Joe by not falling off at his feet?" Liz asked drily as she, too, stood. Natalia handed her a white helmet, then went outside and wheeled the bike down the steps.

"I have to wear a helmet?"

"If you want to ride with Joe, you do."

Liz plopped the helmet on her head, then fastened the chin strap. "I bet I look like a goober with all this hair sticking out."

She didn't expect a response, but Natalia looked her over, then soberly agreed, "Yeah, you do."

After a quick lesson on gears and brakes, Liz climbed onto the bike and peddled between the cottages to the driveway without wobbling too much. The bike's style was retro, looking like something her mother might have ridden forty years ago, with a wide comfortable seat and a design that allowed her to sit upright. Except for the helmet, it was fun, especially when she took a short spin on the paved street, without all the bumps, and she would get used to the helmet.

When she returned to Natalia, she grinned. "I'm not ready to give up my car, but this is cool. Way different from the bike I got for Christmas when I was eight."

"It's not a bad way to get around," Natalia replied.

Liz climbed off and removed the helmet, shaking out her hair. "Maybe I'll settle someplace where I can have a bike."

"I figured you'd settle here. I mean, Joe says he's not going anywhere."

The idea was appealing. So was the possibility that it might appeal to him, too. But sooner or later he'd have to know the truth. While he would be relieved that she'd never had a relationship with his brother, he would be put off by her lies. He would wonder what had been real and what had been calculated to find out Josh's whereabouts. His trust would be damaged.

Or she could stick to her plan: find Josh, drag his butt into court, then return to her job, her reputation restored, her energy directed toward her next assignment. She could try to forget that Joe existed. Try to forget that kiss. To forget the something more that was pretty much destined no matter how they fought it.

The something more that could destroy them.

Or maybe save them.

Chapter 8

Joe was pushing his bike out the rear door of the coffee shop a few minutes past five when Raven appeared in the storeroom door. "Hey, Joe, there's a guy here who wants to talk to you."

Stopping short, he muttered a curse. Two years in this town, and no one had ever come looking for him, and now people were crawling out from under rocks. *Thanks a whole hell of a lot, Josh.*

So far, he'd heard from the ex-girlfriend, the U.S. Attorney's office and the marshals service. Was there another federal office involved, or would this guy be from the Mulroneys? And did he really want to know? Why not just have Raven tell him Joe was already gone?

Because whoever the guy was, it would take him about three minutes to get directions to Joe's house, if not from Raven, then from anyone else in town who knew him. And he did *not* want anyone who worked for the Mulroneys showing up at the house, not with Liz across the yard and Natalia next door.

Griping, he pushed the bike back into the storeroom, locked the door and returned to the dining room. "Nice clothes he's wearing, huh?" Raven murmured as he passed her.

Very nice clothes. Probably five grand for the suit and another thousand for the shoes. Hell, the tie alone could have paid her salary for a month. Yeah, Joe's money would be on the Mulroneys this time.

The man was standing near the wall, studying the foil packs of coffee beans for sale. He picked up one and gave it a sniff before turning it over to read the back.

"You wanted to talk to me?"

He turned and his eyes widened in surprise. "Jeez, when they said *identical,* I didn't really think *identical.*" He extended his hand. "Daniel Wallace. And you're Joe Saldana... right?"

"Yeah. I'm thinking about getting that printed on my shirts."

"Not that anyone would take it as proof." Wallace was black, looked about forty and had a friendly gaze and very good taste in clothes and watches—a Rolex—and even coffee. The bag of Kona he held sold for $42 a pound. "I'm with the firm representing Sean and Patrick Mulroney in their upcoming trial."

"I figured." Though, if he'd really expected someone from the defense side, it would have been some tough guys to intimidate Josh's location from him.

"Everyone's wanting to talk to your brother, aren't they?"

"Everyone but me."

"I can understand that. After all, whoever shot you was aiming for him. But he is still your brother."

"And I still haven't seen him since then. Sorry I can't help you."

He pivoted and took a few steps before Wallace spoke again. "Of course, we'd be happy to help you in return."

Slowly Joe turned and backtracked. Marshal Ashe had theorized that the Mulroneys had paid Josh to disappear, or had used the promise of money to lure him to his death. They probably considered payoffs a necessary cost of doing business, just like coffee and mugs were for him. How much would they be willing to pay *him* for ratting out his brother?

"Help me with what?"

Wallace shrugged. "You have a nice place here, but with only two part-time employees, it must keep you pretty busy. We could assist you with staffing and expenses."

"How much staffing? How many expenses?"

"You want to retire and let someone else run the business for you, we could make that possible. We could see that you get a nice annual income without having to work at all, unless you wanted to."

Retire before thirty-five, live comfortably, and all he had to do was supply information that would get Josh killed.

It was a good thing they'd made this offer to him rather than Josh, because Josh probably would have sold Joe out in a heartbeat.

"I tell you where my brother is, and you take on the expenses of running my business while I reap the profits?" Joe frowned as if concentrating. "Granted, I sell coffee for a living, so I'm not real up on the finer details of law, but there's got to be something illegal in what you're proposing."

"One wouldn't be connected to the other," Wallace said smoothly, and with a straight face. "There's no crime in telling us where your brother is. And there's no crime in the Mulroneys investing in your shop. Their business interests are diversified. This shop would fit nicely into their portfolio."

Lawyers could explain anything so it sounded reasonable

and legal, Joe reflected as he leaned against the nearest table. But a person would have to be blind to not see the connection between him giving up information and being rewarded with an investment in his business. His vision—as well as the U.S. Attorney's—was damn near perfect.

"What do you want with Josh? Just to talk to him, I suppose."

Wallace gestured agreeably.

"To persuade him not to testify or, at least, not to testify truthfully."

"The information he gave the prosecution wasn't truthful. We'd just like him to set the record straight. We want him to admit that he was wrong, or perhaps mistaken, about what he reported."

"What if you found him and he refused to, uh, *set the record straight.* Then what?"

Wallace's smile was even and friendly, and it made Joe think of nothing so much as a predator with its prey in sight. "Then we'd face him in court, of course. Provided he chose to show up. My clients aren't murderers, Mr. Saldana, no matter what the government would have you believe."

"Someone tried to kill me."

"But it wasn't them. Your brother's been involved in illegal dealings since he was sixteen. He's made a lot of enemies of the type far more likely to resort to murder than respectable businessmen such as Sean and Patrick Mulroney."

Joe gazed out the window at the street. There weren't many cars parked out front because most people had already run their Saturday errands. Kids were at the mall, hanging out, and most other folks were probably at home, thinking about dinner or a date or a lazy night in front of the television. Normal things.

Not talking to some investigator trying to convince them that inside was out, up was down and wrong was right.

"I've seen that pretty woman you've been hanging out

with," Wallace said, still in that smooth, easy manner. "You can't convince me you wouldn't like a little more time away from here to spend with her."

A chill spread through Joe at the mention of Liz. They'd finished lunch nearly five hours ago, so Wallace must have been in town at least that long; he must have put off coming here for a reason. To find out more about Joe? More about Liz?

If he said no, would they threaten Liz?

Damn, he was tired of this.

Wallace turned serious. "You almost died because of your brother, and I'm willing to bet he never even said he was sorry. You don't owe him anything."

"I don't owe you or the Mulroneys anything either, and I plan to keep it that way." Joe straightened and gestured toward the door. "Unless you want some coffee, you should leave now."

Deliberately he walked away, though everything in him protested the act of turning his back on Wallace. He circled behind the counter and went to stand beside Raven, who'd made herself a frozen coffee and was sucking it through a straw while flipping through the pages of *People*.

"You going home now?" she asked without looking up.

"Not until he's gone. If he comes back, call the police."

Her gaze jerked up, wide with shock. She looked at Wallace, then at Joe again. "Really? Who is he? What does he want? Are you serious?"

"No, just teasing." He scowled. "Call me, and *I'll* call the police."

Wallace watched them a moment, clearly hearing their conversation. With a shake of his head, he pivoted and walked out the door, climbing into a Mercedes parked outside. He dressed better than the other people looking for Josh, and definitely had better taste in cars—and the money to indulge it. Blood money.

"He's not dangerous," Joe said. *Just a go-between for dangerous people.* "But for real, if he comes back here tonight, call me. And don't tell him *anything.*"

Raven looked almost as pale as she used to when she'd accomplished it with dead-white makeup. "Are you in trouble, Joe?"

A week ago he wouldn't have touched her hair for fear the spikes would cut or the gunk would latch onto his skin like superglue. Now he mussed it, just like he used to do to his girl cousins when they were kids. Just like Josh used to do to him when he called Joe baby brother. "Not me. Don't worry about it, okay? I'll see you Monday."

He walked the bike into the alley and put on his helmet, but instead of heading straight home, he cruised around town for a while, looking for the unfamiliar Mercedes. He was starting to think Wallace had left town when he rode past The Jasmine, Copper Lake's most luxurious place to stay, and saw it parked at the rear of the lot.

Swearing, he headed toward Wyndham Hall.

One of the benefits of riding a bike that had never occurred to him before: It was damn near impossible for someone in a vehicle to follow him unnoticed. No one was lagging behind, and no one drove past and circled the block to pass again. The only cars he saw between The Jasmine and his house were neighbors who belonged on the streets.

When he braked the bike in front of his house, the tension between his shoulders eased a bit. He pushed down the kickstand, then went next door, taking the steps in one stride, knocking at the screen door.

Natalia was on the couch, cell phone to her ear. When she saw him, she raised one finger to him to wait, spoke a few words into the phone, then disconnected and came to undo the hook on the screen. He stepped just inside.

"You didn't have to cut your call short for me," he said.

She shook her head. "I was just ordering a pizza from Luigi's. What's up?"

"Have you seen anyone around here who doesn't belong?"

"Besides your brother's girlfriend, you mean?"

"Ex-girlfriend," he corrected, though there was that damned bit of doubt. At lunch, he'd believed her when she'd said she had no interest in getting back together with Josh, just as he'd believed her when she said she hadn't committed any crimes.

But he hadn't believed her when she'd said someday she would tell him what she wanted from Josh. And now that she wasn't sitting in front of him, looking and sounding so damn sincere, he wasn't sure about the rest.

Honestly, she wasn't the one who could convince him that it was over between her and Josh.

He needed to hear it from Josh.

Everyone's wanting to talk to your brother, Wallace had said, and Joe had responded, *Everyone but me.*

It hadn't taken long to make a liar out of him.

"Ex-girlfriend," Natalia repeated, bringing his attention back to her. Was that skepticism in her voice? Was she just placating him, or was he reading deeper meanings where there were none?

"Have you seen anyone?" he asked again.

She shook her head. "Why?"

He gazed at the television, muted for her pizza order, and recognized the movie playing as a thriller featuring U.S. marshals in search of a fugitive. He'd always thought the suspense and danger were nothing more than the stuff of movies, but here he was, getting visits from marshals and corrupt lawyers and almost run down on the street, and he wasn't even the fugitive.

Maybe Liz had had a taste for danger and excitement, but

he never had. He didn't like looking over his shoulder or being suspicious of every unfamiliar face. He especially didn't like that simply being seen with him might have placed Liz— or Natalia—at risk.

He turned to stare out the door and, of course, his gaze went straight to Liz's house. There was no sign of her, but her car was in its parking space and the front door stood open. He could walk over there, climb the steps, knock at the door, and she would invite him in, and they could…

They could do all kinds of things, some of them very wrong. But they would feel so damn right.

"My brother's in trouble," he said at last, "and a lot of people are looking for him—the U.S. Attorney's office, the U.S. Marshals, and I just finished talking to a lawyer working for the people he's supposed to testify against. These guys have already tried to kill him once, but they shot me instead."

He'd rarely said those words to anyone, so he wasn't sure what reaction he expected, but Natalia's was underwhelming. No shock, no murmurs of sympathy. Getting shot probably wasn't an unusual occurrence in the world she'd come from.

Instead, she moved to stand beside him, her shirt sleeve barely brushing his. Her voice was quiet, controlled. "Do you know where he is?"

He hesitated, then shook his head. After another moment's silence, he murmured, "But I might be able to get in touch with him."

He didn't want to. Truly did not want to talk to Josh ever again. Didn't want to do anything that might lead the feds or the Mulroneys to him. He didn't want any of the responsibility for his brother's fate to fall on him, and he damn sure didn't want to get Josh and Liz together again.

But he could warn Josh to stay away from him and their parents unless he wanted to get caught.

And he could ask him about Liz.

Beside him, Natalia reached out, her fingers resting lightly on the mesh of the screen door. Her nails weren't polished, and her hand looked very small, delicate. "You should do that."

But he *really* didn't want to. "He knows people are looking for him. That's why he's hiding."

"How long do you think he can hide on his own?"

Not long. Joe knew that. So did Liz. Standing on his own two feet was a short-term venture for Josh, at best.

"Get in touch with him, Joe. Find out if he's all right. Convince him to turn himself in." She paused before finishing in a whisper. "He's the only brother you've got."

Convince Josh to turn himself in? He'd have a better shot at making the sun rise in the west. But find out if he was all right…if he was still alive and kicking… And get the okay to go ahead with Liz—or not…

He looked down at Natalia, getting a perfect side profile as she stared ahead. "Do you think his being my brother still matters to me?"

She lifted her gaze to meet his. "Yes, I do. Just like my sisters still matter to me."

Another intimate detail about her. He was surprised by her honesty, and compelled to be just as honest in return. "Yeah. I guess he does."

Although she'd never invited physical contact, on impulse he hugged her, kissed the top of her head, then pushed open the door. "Be careful, Nat. If anything happened to you because of Josh, I'd have to kill him myself." He stepped outside, then closed the door so it didn't bang before finishing.

"And that would probably be a hard thing to live with."

* * *

Liz had wasted too much time after her visit with Natalia watching the clock, waiting for Joe to come home, anticipating…

Him. Seeing him. Talking to him. Being with him.

Anything with him.

It was so juvenile…though if her girlish crushes had ever felt anything like this, she might have stopped beating up boys sooner. She had *so* crossed the line on this one. She shouldn't have a single personal feeling for Joe whatsoever. She shouldn't have let him kiss her. Shouldn't let him set one foot inside this house if he came knocking. Shouldn't let herself cross the lawn and knock at *his* door if he didn't.

She shouldn't care.

But she did. Way too much.

In the kitchen, she opened the refrigerator, then stopped in the act of reaching for a bottle of water. It was wasteful, going through four or five of those a day, then tossing the plastic into the trash without a second thought. And she hadn't even tried the tap water since she'd come here. She'd just assumed bottled had to be better when, truth was, a lot of the time, bottled just came from someone else's tap.

But she'd already bought this case. Not drinking it would be just as wasteful as drinking it, right? As long as she didn't buy more, wouldn't it be more responsible to finish off what was already there?

Taking a bottle, she twisted off the cap and swallowed a big gulp. As she returned to the living room, her cell phone rang from its place on the sofa cushion. She picked it up as she dropped down, making the wicker creak. "Hello, Mika."

"Guess who's in Copper Lake? Daniel Wallace."

"Lawyer to Chicago's rich and indicted?"

"That's him. He paid a visit to Joe at the coffee shop."

"How do you know that?" As far as she knew, she was the only good guy in town keeping an eye on Joe, and obviously, the information hadn't come from her. "Is Ashe still in town?"

"Yeah, coincidentally. He stuck around a while after talking to you guys to meet up with a friend from Augusta. He was leaving a restaurant after a late lunch when he saw Wallace and recognized him from the file photos."

"Is Ashe headed back to Atlanta?"

"Yes, but before leaving, he followed Wallace to a B & B called The Jasmine. You know it?"

"I've seen it. I can't afford it on what I get paid." It was a gorgeous mansion a few blocks from downtown, restored to its prewar glory. Only people with money stayed at The Jasmine. Everyone else hit one of the cheaper motels.

"Keep an eye out for the guy. And find out from Joe what he wanted."

What he wanted was obviously Josh. Had he tried to buy Josh's location from Joe? Or to scare it out of him? "I will."

"How did he react to Ashe's visit?"

Liz blew out her breath. "He was a little hostile. I don't blame him."

"He can blame his brother," Mika said unsympathetically.

"Hey, you know what they say. You can choose your friends, but you can't choose your family."

"You can break all ties with them."

Was that what Mika had done? In the years Liz had known her, she'd never heard a single reference to a mother or father, sister or brother. But then, Mika had always been very private. She could be married and paying a nanny to raise a dozen children, for all Liz knew.

"Find out what you can from Joe and get back to me."

"I will." Liz disconnected, then turned to look out the

window. Joe's black bike was parked on the porch of his house. He'd slipped in while she wasn't looking.

It was nearly six-thirty. If he was tired from working late, maybe she could persuade him to go out to dinner with her.

Or to spend a quiet evening at home with her.

Either of which could bring them closer to what she really wanted.

It was wrong. It could damage her career. It could break her heart. But she wanted it anyway. Wanted him.

His blinds were drawn, but light shone around the edges. Was he showering away the sweet coffee aromas that he'd breathed in all day? Getting a beer from the refrigerator? Kicking back watching someone somewhere play baseball?

Was he thinking of her at all?

She went into the bathroom, stripped off her clothes and took a shower, then dried and dressed in her sexiest underwear, a lacy cream-colored bra and panties, what there was of them, that matched. Standing in front of the closet, she considered the clothes she'd brought with her. Jeans and T-shirt would be the wise choice, the baggy ones that she wore around the house when she didn't even bother to fix her hair.

But when she reached for an outfit, it wasn't that one. Instead, she pulled out a red dress. It was nothing special, buttoning up the front and falling to the knee, sleeveless and snug-fitting and perfectly suitable for the office, a restaurant, even a church. She slid her arms into it and fastened the buttons, stopping one from the bottom, then let her hair down, loosening the curls with her fingers. Foundation, eye shadow, mascara, lipstick, a spritz of perfume, and she was almost ready.

The last detail stood on the floor in the closet: red heels with white polka dots and a matching bow. High heels, four inches, nicely naughty. Joe was a leg man with a bit of a fetish for a woman in heels. She would take every advantage she could get.

She turned off the bedroom light, stopped in the living room for her cell and purse, then went outside, pausing long enough to lock the door. As she turned, light appeared across the way: Joe had opened his door and was standing there, silhouetted against the screen. She couldn't make out his features or his clothes, but she knew it was him. Knew he was watching her.

It's not too late. She could go back inside, or walk around the house to her car and drive away. She could go to dinner or to a club. She could find someone to share a drink with, to dance with, to take her mind off Joe.

But her mind hadn't been completely off Joe in the two-plus years since they'd met.

She took a breath. Went down the steps and to the edge of the sidewalk. Took off her heels. Walked barefoot through the cool grass to the edge of the second sidewalk. Put the heels back on. Climbed his steps.

He turned on the porch light but made no move to open the screen door. The faint scents of soap and shampoo drifted on the air, and his hair was slicked back, his feet bare. He wore khaki shorts that displayed an impressive pair of muscular legs, and a T-shirt, old, faded, bearing only part of a logo for the University of Illinois. The rest had flaked away in years of wear.

He looked incredible.

"Hey." His voice was low, husky.

"Hey," she echoed, just as soft and husky.

"You look…" He sucked in a breath and shifted as if standing still had become uncomfortable. "I was going to come over."

"Should I go back home and wait?"

Finally he raised one hand to the screen door and pushed it open. "No," he said with a grin that made her knees go weak. "Come in."

She was careful not to bump him as she went inside, though she swore she felt the heat and tension radiating from him. A few steps into the room, she stopped, both hands clutching her purse, and faced him. "I wondered if I could talk you into going to dinner with me."

"Dinner?" he echoed.

"To start."

He considered it, as if there were many things he'd rather do at the moment than sit in a restaurant, eat and make polite conversation. Some of them, she was pretty sure, were things she'd prefer as well. "Okay," he said. "Let me change clothes."

"You can go like that." He had great legs, and the T-shirt was snug enough to prove that his chest and arms were hard-muscled as well.

"With you looking like that? No, thanks." He strode down the hall toward his bedroom, leaving her alone in the living room.

She wanted to just stand there, or take a seat, the way any woman waiting for a man to change clothes would. She wanted to consider the evening ahead and all its possibilities. Would dinner be comfortable, tense, romantic? Would he be interested in going for a drink afterward? Would he want to prolong their time together? Walk her to her door? Kiss her? Accept her invitation to come inside?

She *didn't* want to look around the living room, searching for hiding places. She didn't want to plan how to get him to confide the details of Daniel Wallace's visit. She didn't want to ask any questions or assess any answers for veracity or deception.

She wanted a simple dinner date with the man she was wildly attracted to. No job, no lies, no role-playing.

Listening to footsteps, then running water, she circled the couch to the bookcases. There was no desk in the living room, no file cabinet, no address book left carelessly on a table. Maybe he kept his personal records in the bedroom, in a closet or in the office at the coffee shop. What she was looking for—an address, a phone number, an e-mail address—could be concealed in so many ways that a thorough search might never reveal it. A note tucked inside the covers of a book or the case of a DVD. Information disguised as an account number. Data written in code. It could also have been memorized and destroyed. She could be searching for something that existed only in Joe's brain.

Sighing, she flipped through the magazines stacked on the bookcase. *Green Gourmet. Organic Grounds. Going Green for Small Businesses. Sustainability.* Fascinating reading, she was sure. The bottom one was a glossy biking magazine touting Rocky Mountain views from a bike seat. The guy on the cover wore skin-tight clothing that displayed muscled calves to make a woman drool.

"Where do you—"

Liz turned as Joe broke off. He'd changed into gray trousers and a white shirt, tucked in, sleeves rolled up to just below his elbows. There was no way around it. The man was hot no matter what he wore.

She held up the magazine. "You planning a vertical bike trip through Colorado?"

His gaze shifted to the magazine and held for a moment before he shrugged casually. "It's on my list of things to do. Are you ready, or would you rather read an interesting article on the most expensive coffee in the world? It's in the top magazine in your right hand. They feed the coffee cherries to civets, then collect the beans after they pass through their digestive system. They say it's very good. Sells for about $50 a cup."

"After they pass through… Eww." Suspiciously, she looked from him to the magazine. "You made that up."

"Scout's honor." He crossed to her side, slid the *Organic*

Grounds issue from her grip and flipped it open to a picture of a weasely-looking critter.

She scanned the article, then shoved all the magazines into his hands. "That's just gross. Way more organic than I ever want to know about."

He put the magazines away, then gestured toward the door. "I'm guessing you're not walking far in those ridiculous—"

She shot him a look over her shoulder.

"—ly sexy heels, so we're taking your car?"

"You can even drive if you want. If you remember how."

"It hasn't been that long," he replied drily as he locked the door.

"That's right. You borrow Mrs. Wyndham's car for mysterious trips that you won't talk about."

"If I talked about them, they wouldn't be mysterious, would they?"

She went through the heels-off-to-cross-the-grass routine again, then handed him the car keys. After opening the passenger door for her, he slid behind the wheel, adjusting the seat for his longer legs, then the mirrors and the steering wheel.

"Have you been to Chantal's?" he asked as he backed out.

"No." She'd seen it downtown, in the corner of a retail center tucked between River Road and the river, and thought it seemed more a couples kind of place.

"Good."

Liz let a few blocks pass in silence, simply enjoying the moment, before taking a silent breath and asking, "How was the rest of your day? Any more distractions?"

For a time Joe's gaze remained fixed on the street ahead. His hands were relaxed on the wheel, but his jaw was clenched. Finally, he glanced her way. "Yeah. One. A lawyer from Chicago. The Mulroneys want to invest in the coffee shop."

"So if the money-laundering business dries up, they'll have

something to fall back on. And, totally separate from that, of course, you'll just happen to volunteer your brother's location."

He nodded.

She gazed out the window, watching houses give way to businesses. No doubt about it. Daniel Wallace had balls. Approaching a witness's brother so openly, and doing it himself rather than sending an underling so he could maintain deniability… Overconfidence? Faith that Josh wasn't going to show up in court?

Maybe the Mulroneys *knew* Josh wasn't going to testify because they'd had him killed. Maybe Wallace had come himself because, once Josh's body was discovered, he could claim innocence for his clients. *We were trying to locate Josh Saldana. Would we have bothered if we'd known he was dead?*

Josh was a pain in the butt, a petty criminal, a sweet-talking charmer, irresponsible, infuriating, dishonest. But he was Joe's brother. Dory and Ruben Saldana's son. He deserved a lot, starting with a stint in prison and a megadose of reality, but he didn't deserve to die.

The parking lot that fronted Chantal's was full, so Joe parked on the street across the square from Ellie's Deli. As they waited at the curb for a break in traffic on River Road, a car filled with teenage boys stopped to let them cross.

"Hey, chica, you look hot," the front-seat passenger called. "Why don't you come with us? We show you a good time."

Liz gave him her brightest smile. Beside her, Joe frowned and took her hand. "Those boys wouldn't know what to do with you," he muttered.

"Sometimes neither do you."

"I know what to do *with* you. It's what to do *about* you that I can't figure."

As they approached the hot-red awning that sheltered Chantal's entrance, her hand warm and secure inside his, Liz understood exactly what he meant.

Chapter 9

After a twenty-minute wait for a table, Joe and Liz ordered their meals—his shrimp and scallops, hers fried catfish. They were seated on the deck that looked across the river, with torches providing flickering light. The scent of jasmine was heavy on the air, and water lapped at the shore. Turn up the heat, add some sand and a pitcher of piña coladas, and he could almost imagine a tropical paradise.

If he drank the whole pitcher first.

Liz leaned forward, arms resting on the wicker tabletop. "So tell me about this trip to Colorado."

For an instant he drew a blank, but quickly the lie came back. When he'd gone into the living room and seen her holding the magazine—*the* magazine, the one he'd given so much thought to in the past few days—he'd gone cold. His first impulse had been to grab it out of her hands and hide it someplace far out of her reach. He'd even started toward her, but sense had kicked in before she'd been within grabbing range.

"It's just something I've thought about," he lied. Sure, he liked riding his bike, both for environmental reasons and because it was fun. But riding in Copper Lake, Georgia, elevation 150 feet, was a whole other world from Colorado's 8,000 to 12,000-foot peaks. Building muscle on top of muscle in his legs and starving his lungs weren't his idea of fun.

But he had to credit Josh with picking the right magazine to send his message. No one who knew him would give it a second thought. It was the sort of thing people expected to find in his house.

"You're more ambitious than I am. I love the mountains, but riding a bike up and down one…" Settling back in her chair, she fanned her face languorously. "Makes me weak just to think about it."

She was so gorgeous, relaxed, her curls shifting lightly in the breeze, so strong. She'd never seemed less *weak* in all the time he'd known her. He, on the other hand, was feeling pretty damn helpless. All he wanted to do was look at her, touch her, kiss her, make love to her. Forever.

"It's going up the mountain that's tough." His voice was husky, scratchy. "Coming down's just a matter of holding on."

"What if you lose control?"

"You don't let that happen."

"But what if you do?"

They weren't talking about bikes and mountains anymore. What *would* happen when they lost control? Who would be first to recover? Who would have the most to recover from? He wasn't looking to get his heart broken, but if he was going to spend the next few years regretting something, better that it be something he did than something he didn't do.

He'd already spent a long time regretting that he didn't kiss her that night in Josh's kitchen.

He made a stab at a smile. "Then you hold on tight while you look for a soft place to fall."

She held his gaze a long time, but didn't say anything. He couldn't think of anything to say.

The waitress delivered their food, and they did the small-talk chatter that reminded him of too many first dates, when they were way past that stage. After clearing the table, the waitress offered coffee.

They declined, and ten minutes later, after refusing Liz's offer to pay, he was putting his wallet back in his hip pocket as he followed her through the restaurant to the door. It was a brief but most enjoyable journey. That ass, those legs, damn, those shoes... He wanted to make love to her while she wore those and nothing else.

And he was going to. Maybe tonight, maybe tomorrow, but definitely soon. It was either that or go totally freaking insane.

The night was cool as they strolled the sidewalk that curved around to the road, but Liz, in her sleeveless dress, didn't seem to mind. *Hot-blooded,* Josh had described her.

Even thinking of his brother wasn't enough to cool the need pulsing through him. As they approached the intersection, he took her hand. The first time it had been more of a claiming act, letting the smart-mouthed kid know she was with *him.* This time he did it because he needed to touch her. Because it felt good. Because, hell, she was with *him.*

"Thank you for dinner."

He glanced at her from the corner of his eye—a blur of olive skin, black curls, red dress. "You're welcome."

"Can I buy you a drink someplace?"

He did look at her then, her eyes intense, expectant and cautious, before checking his watch. "No, thanks. But I'll teach you how to make a killer cup of coffee if you'd like." It was five after nine, and Raven was always gone by five till. Only the usual night-lights showed in the shop, offering them privacy as well as the best coffee in town.

Some women could be seduced by fine food, others by fine wine or cheap booze. Liz, he was pretty sure, could be seduced by fine coffee. He damn well knew *he* could be.

She smiled, and the caution faded from her gaze. "I would like that very much."

They jaywalked through the square at a diagonal, coming out in front of the shop. He unlocked the door, then locked up again behind them. Still holding her hand, he led her behind the counter, then through the door into the storeroom, switching on only the light above the corner counter.

The space was small and cramped, but he could find anything he needed in no time. Dropping his hand, Liz turned in a circle, taking in his desk and file cabinet, sofa, cupboards and storage shelves. Everything there was recycled, reusable or came from renewable resources. "I expected great big bins of coffee. Where is it?"

"I get deliveries from a roastery in Augusta every day or two. Coffee starts to deteriorate right after it's roasted. That's why the mass-produced stuff on the grocery shelves doesn't taste so hot. For the best coffee, you need fresh-roasted single-estate high-grown Arabica beans—" he held up the foil bag he'd opened that morning "—a burr grinder, cold filtered water and a machine. At home I usually use a French press, but because I don't have a burner here to boil the water, I use an electric machine. It's almost as good and very simple." He beckoned to her. "Come here."

Liz went to stand beside him, her perfume a sweet and spicy counterpoint to the beans' rich, earthy aroma. He pulled her closer and wrapped her fingers around the measuring cup.

"The ideal ratio is considered fifty-five grams of ground coffee to a liter of cold filtered water, but we're doing only one cup and, like everything else, coffee has to be adjusted to your personal preferences." He gestured to the sink on the right. "I'm going to show you my preferences."

She turned on the faucet, filled the eight-ounce cup and carefully emptied it into the reservoir at the top of the coffee maker. Next came the grinder. "You grind it fresh for every cup?"

"Always."

She took the foil-lined bag, unfastened it and drew a deep breath. "Mmm. Wonderful." With her eyes closed, the dreamy expression on her face and the huskiness of her voice, she looked and sounded wonderful. She made him ache, but sometimes hurting felt good. "Is this single-estate, high-grown Arabica?"

"It is. It comes from El Salvador and is a blend of two very old Arabicas—Bourbon and Typica. The *cafétos,* or coffee trees, are grown at a thousand meters or higher on shade-covered hills. That makes the bean smaller." He moved to stand behind her. "Denser." Close enough now to smell the faint fragrance of her perfume. "Sweeter."

Close enough that all she had to do was lean back an inch, maybe two, to bring their bodies together. Close enough that he could feel the heat radiating from her. The need.

She drew another breath, a trying-to-regain-control sort of breath. "So I pour the beans in here?"

"Hmm."

"How much?"

He brushed his mouth against her hair and awareness rippled between them. "Just a few. Until I tell you to stop."

Her hand trembled as she raised the bag over the grinder. She shook out the beans, two or three at a time, enough for three cups before he remembered to say stop. "That's enough. Now pulse the beans."

She lowered her hand to the base of the machine, but did nothing until he covered it with his own hand, guiding her index finger to the button, pressing it. The rattle of beans against burr was harsh, but it didn't distract him. Like Pavlov's dog, the sound of the coffee grinder never failed to make him eager for a taste, and tonight was no exception. Except it wasn't Topéca Manzano he wanted to taste.

How had it gotten so warm in here? Liz wondered. The temperature must have risen by at least ten degrees in the past few minutes. Her body was hot. Her skin was damp. Even her hair was feeling the heat. She wanted to strip off her clothes, to strip off Joe's, to get even hotter.

But all in good time…and this coffee-making lesson was definitely a good time.

He shifted until they were touching, his arms around her, his focus still—at least, partly—on the lesson. "You want to break up most of the bean so that more of it's exposed to the brewing process. But if you grind it too fine, it'll wash through the filter." His mouth was near her ear now, soft rough sounds and warm breaths that made her shiver despite the fever burning through her.

She eased the tension holding her stiff and sagged, just a little, against him. Immediately he moved even closer, and immediately his arousal nudged against her. Her knees went weak at the sensation.

With great effort she tried to concentrate on her task, though she doubted she would remember any of the instructions in an hour's time.

"The coffee grounds go here." He opened a small, cone-shaped projection on the machine. "More than a tablespoon, less than a heaping tablespoon."

Her hand shook as she scooped up the grounds, and he steadied it as he guided the spoon to the filter.

"Now close it."

They did that together.

"Put the cup here."

She took a ceramic cup from the rack next to the sink and placed it under the filter.

"And turn it on here." Again his hand guided hers. "And in four and a half minutes or so, you'll have an excellent cup of coffee."

She stared at the small red float bobbing in the water reservoir as the machine started to work. "Four and a half minutes? What do we do while we wait?"

"Gee, I don't know." His voice was husky, aroused and amused as he settled his hands at her middle, then slid them slowly up, across her midriff, then her breasts, to the top button. "Get you out of that dress, maybe?"

Lowering her gaze, she watched his long, slender fingers deftly slide the first button free, then the second. He was in no hurry, taking his sweet time, grazing his fingers across exposed skin, raising goose bumps, making her breath catch. Her eyes drifting shut, she let her head fall back to rest on his shoulder, and he took advantage of it by pressing a kiss to her temple.

"You are so beautiful," he murmured as his fingers skimmed across her belly, seeking the next button. One more, maybe two, and she could shrug out of the dress, let it slide over her hips and fall to the floor. That would leave her in nothing but barely-there lingerie, and would leave her no choice but to remove Joe's clothes as well.

She was looking forward to it.

Major understatement. She went liquid inside at the thought of getting her hands on him.

The coffee machine sputtered and hissed as the last of the water ran through. The fragrance was lush, intoxicating.

"Nice aroma," Joe murmured, nipping at her ear lobe, tickling around her belly button. "Excellent body. Complex flavor. Sweet aftertaste." He punctuated the words with kisses along her jaw, turning her in his arms so he could explore further.

"Are you talking about me or the coffee?"

With one last great sizzle, the coffeemaker shut off, and in the silence, Joe stared at her, his blue gaze intense, just a little bit troubled. He didn't want to do this. She knew because she didn't either. Wrong as it was, though—reckless, unprofessional, risky—she couldn't walk away. If he could…

She wrapped her arms around his neck and, for a moment, just held him tightly. "We'll deal with it later," she whispered, her voice very nearly soundless in the quiet. "But right now… please, Joe…"

Giving up on words, she kissed him and, for just a moment, he let her, unresponsive, still. Abruptly, he pulled her hard against him, her dress forgotten, his hands cupping her bottom, rubbing her against his erection while his tongue thrust inside her mouth.

It had been way too long since she'd been so hungry for a kiss that she couldn't bear to break it to remove her clothes. Clinging to him, she shimmied out of her dress and left it, a bright spot of red on the industrial gray carpet. Bodies twined together, soft moans mingled with shallow breaths, they moved blindly from the cabinet a half dozen feet to the sofa.

With far less finesse and patience than he'd shown, she yanked loose the buttons on his shirt, pulled it free from his pants and shoved it halfway down his arms, then left him to discard it while she unbuckled his belt, then undid his trousers. Plastic crinkled an instant before they landed on the floor, along with her bra and panties, joined a second later by his boxers.

She'd recognized that crinkling sound—a condom wrapper—and smiled faintly. He might have his doubts about the wisdom of this, but he'd come prepared anyway. He wasn't walking away.

The couch was soft, sturdy, creaking only a bit under their combined weight. With her hands and her mouth and soft, helpless whimpers, Liz urged him to hurry with the condom, to forget about caressing and exploring and everything else— this time, at least—to just slide inside her and fill her, complete her, bring her some relief.

And when he did, when he was cradled deep inside her, when they were as close physically as two people could ever be, she realized that it didn't matter—that she was being un-professional, that she was on the job, that she was deceiving him, that he was likely to break her heart. Whatever happened the next day, the next week, the next month, she would have this to get her through it.

This one night with Joe would be worth whatever conse-quences she would have to face. One night of intimacy. One night of knowing he cared for her whether he wanted to or not. One night of acknowledging that she felt the same for him, whether she wanted to or not. One night.

Damned if she wouldn't make it the best night.

"Damn."

Joe's soft curse was the first coherent word either of them had spoken since Liz had whispered, *Please, Joe...* It was im-possible to tell whether the emotion behind it was anger, regret, pleasure or some combination of the three. Her response, if she made one, would be purely pleasure. She had no anger and certainly no regret.

Even though what she'd just done might have been a career-ending move.

Even though there was no future for the two of them.

She was lying on the couch, facing the desk, Joe snuggled close behind her. Because he wanted to be close? Or there wasn't any space to put between them? Her heart was still thudding, her skin still flushed, her toes still curled, but she could breathe now. In the instant before the first orgasm—or was it the second?—she'd thought she was going to pass out from lack of air. Her lungs had been constricted, her heart pounding, her body wired, tight, as sensation spiraled through her out of control.

Wouldn't that have been a hoot? Her first sex in far too long and her passed out from too much pleasure before it was finished.

With no windows in the storeroom, it was impossible to tell how much time had passed. She could lift her head and check Joe's watch, but that seemed too much effort. It had been time enough to make love twice—three times if she counted that first frantic coupling separately from the slow, lazy, sensual journey it had led to.

Time enough to make her face one fact: She didn't have to worry about getting her heart broken sometime in the future. It was cracking even as she lay there, warm and sweaty and sated, in Joe's arms.

It wasn't fair. She'd waited too long to want a man this way, far too long to feel this way about a man. Why did it have to be *this* man?

Because sometimes life was good, and sometimes it bit you on the ass.

"Liz."

Here it comes. The jeez-this-was-a-mistake, we'll-pretend-it-never-happened-and-make-sure-it-never-happens-again speech. She steeled herself for it—hard to do when she was lying there naked, skin to skin with him. But she forced the best answer she could. "Hmm?"

"We should probably go."

She wanted to protest that she hadn't had her coffee yet, but he didn't wait for a response before levering himself over her and onto his feet. Turning his back to her, he pulled on his boxers, then his trousers. By the time she sat up and retrieved her underwear from the floor, he was sliding his feet into his shoes and tucking in his shirt. By the time she finished buttoning her dress, he'd thrown away the coffee, emptied the grounds into a bucket next to the door and unplugged the machine.

He was definitely feeling some regret.

The odds of getting him to talk about what they'd done were somewhere between slim and none, so as she passed the bucket, she gestured to it. "What do you do with the grounds?"

He blinked as if she'd spoken in a foreign tongue, then focused on the pail. "I give them away. Miss Abigail, Sara Calloway and Lydia Kennedy use them in their gardens. They provide as much nitrogen as fertilizer but are more eco-friendly, and they're great for acid-loving plants, like azaleas. Plus, worms love coffee grounds."

"And that's good?" she asked as he none-too-subtly moved her into the shop proper and toward the door.

"Worms aerate the soil, which allows good root formation." At the front entrance, he glanced up and down the street before turning the key in the lock, then ushering her outside. "There's also some evidence that the use of coffee grounds is helpful in repelling gophers and moles."

Worms, gophers and moles. She'd never had a sillier conversation so soon after having great sex. But silly talk was better than no talk at all. It was better than the mistake speech she'd been expecting. Was still expecting.

The night was humid, quiet and cool. Her car was the only one parked on the square. Every business was closed up, everyone gone home. "What time is it?" she asked as they walked toward Ellie's Deli.

"Twelve-twenty."

His hands were at his sides. It would be so easy to slip her hand into his, curl her fingers over his. He probably wouldn't push her away. He probably wouldn't do anything at all— would just tolerate her action—and for that reason, she did nothing either.

She tried conversation again. "Do you think Natalia let Elizabeth and Bear out?"

"I'm sure she did."

"So they won't be bouncing up and down with their legs crossed by the time you get there."

At the corner they turned south, walking along the western edge of the square. He breathed deeply—wishing she would just shut up and let him regret in silence?—and said, "No. They're probably kicked back on the sofa, if they haven't destroyed it, watching Animal Planet."

"Geez, they eat one pillow and get branded as destructive for life. Cut 'em some slack. It was one mistake." As she faced him across the car, she lowered her voice. "Cut yourself some slack, Joe."

For the first time, he met her gaze, his mouth a thin line. He started to speak, then shook his head and unlocked the doors.

What had he been about to say? That having sex with her was a mistake he wouldn't make again? That he wanted to forget it ever happened? She would give almost anything if he'd insist that it hadn't been a mistake at all. That he still wanted her. That he would always want her.

Of course he didn't.

She gave in to silence on the way home, feeling bluer with each passing block. When he parked next to her house, she got out and picked her way carefully over uneven ground to the sidewalk. Feeling the chill more acutely, she lengthened her stride, climbed the steps and stuck the key into the lock.

"You think it was a mistake?"

Joe's voice came from behind her. Slowly she turned to face him. He stood at the bottom of the steps, serious, still, unbearably handsome.

In every way. "No."

"Neither do I." He sounded as sincere as she did. Was he lying, too?

"Then what…?"

He dragged his fingers through his hair before shrugging and parroting an answer she'd given him a few days earlier. "It's complicated."

Her laughter was short and regretful. "With you Saldana boys, everything's complicated."

"See, that's part of the problem. Most women I date don't even know I have a brother. You know. Man, do you *know.*"

If life were fair, she would tell him the truth: that Josh had never laid a hand on her unless it was for an audience. The bigger truth: that she'd never wanted him to. The biggest truth of all: that she'd never wanted any man the way she wanted *him.*

She returned to the top step and gazed down at him. "But I'm not holding it against you."

Against his will, he laughed before sobering. "It's just… weird. You being with Josh for so long, then tonight with me. It's…"

Weird, she agreed. If it were true. When he was physically identical to the ex-boyfriend, it would be hard not to wonder if he was being used as a substitute, if when she touched him, kissed him, made love to him, she imagined he was Josh instead of Joe.

"I can honestly say I didn't think of Josh even for an instant tonight."

Joe stared at her, still, as if he didn't believe her.

"What do you want me to say, Joe? That I wish I'd never known Josh? That I'd never been involved with him?" To counteract a shiver, she folded her arms across her middle so her hands were tucked against what little warmth her body had to offer. "I've told you before—I don't love Josh and never did. I don't want him back. Everything between us is over. Once I find him, I won't care if I never see him again."

"And what about everything between *us*?" Joe asked quietly. "Once you find Josh, what happens to us?"

She didn't know what to say. How could she commit to a relationship with him when he didn't know who she really was? How could she promise him anything? She didn't even know what she wanted. A long-distance affair? To see where weekend visits, sex and e-mail could take them? Was she willing to give up her job and live in Copper Lake? Would she rather lure him to Dallas or some other city?

She didn't have a clue what she wanted…besides him. Romance, love, marriage, family—the whole fantasy would be incredible. But maybe they'd find out in a few months' time that the attraction between them was mostly physical, and they'd each be ready to move on. Maybe they cared, but not enough to make a long-term commitment work.

She could give up her career for a sure thing, but for nothing more than maybes?

"I guess silence is a pretty clear answer, isn't it?" Clouds had drifted over the moon, throwing his face into shadow, but she heard the disappointment in his voice.

"No, Joe, that isn't—"

But he'd already pivoted and headed toward his house, his long legs taking long strides. She could kick off her shoes and run after him. She could yell across the space to him.

But she chose to do the wise thing: let him go. She stood

there in the cool night shadows and watched until he disappeared inside the lavender house. Watched his shadow pass
the window. Watched moment after moment while everything
remained still.

Her feet hurting, her skin cold, her chest tight, she heaved
a sigh at last and turned to the door. Just before she went
inside, she cast another glance across the lawn and murmured,
"That's not my answer at all."

Joe had trouble falling asleep. His yawns were so wide that
they swallowed his face, but he couldn't relax enough. Liz's
fragrance clung to his skin, even after a 2:00 a.m. shower. His
fingers tingled with the feel of her. His whole self echoed with
her silence.

What about us?

When he finally drifted off, it was to disjointed dreams of
Liz, him, Josh, pain and disappointment and loss.

He got up at seven, groggy and still tired, and put the dogs
out. There was no sign of life across the yard.

After letting the pups in again, he set out food dishes and fresh
water in the middle of the kitchen floor, then fell back into bed,
back into a restless sleep. It was nearly noon when he awoke
again. His head hurt. His eyes felt like sandpaper. His joints were
stiff. He couldn't remember the last time he'd slept in so late, or
the last time he'd woken up feeling so lousy. College, probably.

Beside him, Elizabeth lifted her head, scowling her annoyance with him for disturbing her nap. He scowled back, slid
to his feet and shuffled into the kitchen. First things first:
dumping Ayutepeque beans into the grinder, scooping more
than a tablespoon but less than a heaping tablespoon into the
filter, adding eight ounces of cold water from the refrigerator
dispenser. While the coffee perked, he went into the living
room and returned with the biking magazine.

It had arrived in the mail two months ago, give or take, in a manila envelope postmarked Denver. The address had been handwritten with a felt-tip marker, by a woman, he'd guess. It would have been so easy for Josh to persuade a postal clerk to do it—a phony bandage on his right hand, a smile, *Please.* Anything to keep the feds from recognizing his writing—and Joe, too, because he probably would have thrown it away unopened if he'd known it was from Josh.

He'd almost tossed it anyway, figuring it was junk mail, a come-on from someone who wanted to part him from his money. But he'd flipped through the pages, and near the back a familiar mark had caught his attention. A smudge on the final digit of the page number. A printer's error, or so it seemed.

It was a simple code, one they'd used as kids, when age and proximity had kept them close. Anything with numbers and letters worked—a book, a newspaper, a catalog. Small smudges, faint pencil lines, blots—the message was spelled out one letter or digit at a time. He'd written this one down the night he'd gotten it, then immediately burned the paper. Now he wrote it down again.

For emergency. Following it was a ten-digit number.

How had Josh gotten his address? had been his first thought. From their mother's friend, Opal, maybe. Hell, he might have looked up Joe on the Internet. *Leave it to the good brother to hide using his real name,* he could imagine Josh scoffing.

What emergency could ever make Joe want to contact him? had been his next thought. Nothing less tragic than the death of one of their parents.

That and, now, Liz.

What about us?

Her damned silence still rang in his ears.

Did it matter now whether Josh still had a claim on her? No. Because, apparently, Joe didn't either.

But maybe… Maybe then he'd know whether she'd been using him as a substitute for Josh.

The coffee finished, and he breathed deeply, immediately regretting it. Damned if it didn't make him remember last night. Damned if it didn't arouse him more than a little. Great. Getting a hard-on every time he smelled coffee brewing, especially when he worked in a freaking coffee shop… He'd known Liz was trouble from the first time he'd seen her. Had known he should stay the hell away from her. But no, he'd had to ignore the wise voices in his head, and look at him now.

He sweetened the coffee with a spoonful of raw sugar, then drank it while he got dressed, laced on his sneakers, took his helmet from the coat stand. With the notepaper crinkling, he stuffed his wallet in one pocket, a handful of change in another, grabbed his keys and left the house.

He needed a pay phone because it seemed likely that his home, cell and shop phones were being monitored by the good guys, the bad guys or maybe both. And the best place to use a pay phone unnoticed was at the mall.

He carried the bike down the steps and was cinching the helmet strap tightly when he caught the sound of a door closing nearby. *Not Liz,* he thought, hoped grimly, but of course it was.

With her hair in a ponytail, khaki shorts and a short-sleeved chambray shirt, she should have looked as casual as hell. She didn't. She looked beautiful and elegant—there were creases pressed into her shorts, for pity's sake—and uncharacteristically uncomfortable. "Hi."

He nodded curtly as he mounted the bike.

"I, uh, wondered if we were still on for our ride to the lake today. Natalia said I could, uh, borrow her bike."

He'd made the suggestion less than forty-eight hours earlier, just before some thug had tried to run them down on the sidewalk. It had seemed a good idea then—a nice place, a picnic lunch, a pretty woman… Now he couldn't think of much he wanted less than private time with Liz. "Later, okay?"

"Oh. Okay." She shifted, her sandaled feet coming into view in the grass where he was staring. She sounded part disappointed, part phony. "I can give you a ride wherever you're going."

"No, thanks."

"I don't mind. We could talk."

Oh yeah, that sounded like fun. He'd tried talking last night, hadn't he, and look where it'd gotten him. "Look, I'm not in much of a mood for talking. Maybe later." *Maybe never.*

Her cheeks flushed and she took a step back. She tried to smile, but it was shaky. "Okay. Sure. Later."

She watched as he rode away. He swore he could feel her gaze on him long after distance and Miss Abigail's house had blocked her view.

It was good weather for riding: sunny, not too hot or too humid, just enough breeze to cool without affecting control of the bike. He hardly noticed it, though. His attention was focused on the upcoming call.

He would tell Josh to stay away from the Mulroneys, from their parents, from him.

He would ask what was between Josh and Liz.

He would ask what she wanted from him.

He would ask why he shouldn't give her the phone number.

And he would tell his brother, if he bothered to ask, that their parents were fine.

And to be careful.

Assuming, of course, that the number was still good, that he got to talk to Josh at all, that his brother was even alive to talk to.

Hands tight on the grips, Joe waited for a break in traffic, then turned left onto Carolina Avenue. The mall was a half dozen blocks to the east, small, one-story, sitting in the middle of a six-acre parking lot. There were no bike racks, so when he stopped near the main entrance, he climbed off and secured the bike to a light post with the chain and padlock he kept looped around the crossbar.

The air inside was cool, processed, stale. The food court was busy, shoppers moved from store to store, and kids congregated wherever there was room. A good chunk of Copper Lake still believed that Sunday was the Lord's day and ate dinner with family after church, but the rest of them were shopping or hanging out here.

Holding his helmet by the strap, he headed toward the little-used south entrance, where a small alcove just inside the doors housed two pay phones and an ATM. Turning his back to the shoppers, he dug the number from his pocket, dropped in two quarters and, with hardly a tremble to his hand, he dialed.

At the other end, the phone rang four times before going to voice mail. The recording was to the point: "Leave a message." It was Josh's voice, not so flippant, not so smug as usual, but proof that two months ago, at least, he'd been alive.

Before Joe found his voice, the phone disconnected. He fed in two more quarters, dialed again and this time, after the beep, said, "It's me. Joe. I'm at a pay phone at 706-555-3312. I'll hang around here for ten minutes. If you don't call, I'll try again later."

When he hung up, his palm was sweaty. He dried it on his jeans, then turned to gaze across the open area of the mall. The nearest store on the left was a clothing boutique that catered to well-dressed toddlers, dressing them like miniature versions of their well-heeled parents. Directly across from it was a sporting goods place, and in the middle stood a jewelry kiosk. Listening to seconds ticking off slowly in his head, he scanned the people sitting on couches just past the kiosk, recognizing a few of his regular customers before movement drew his gaze back to the jewelry. It hadn't been much—a swing of black curls lassoed into a ponytail—and he was sure there were other women in town with curly black hair even if he couldn't think of any offhand.

Then the clerk inside the kiosk moved, and Joe's gaze locked with Liz's. The look on her face was funny—grim, resigned, guilty—and brought with it a numb realization: She had followed him.

And it wasn't because she wanted to talk about last night. Oh, she was talking, all right, to whoever was on the cell phone. He was too far away to hear any of her conversation, but he had a sick feeling in his gut that it was about him.

His chest was tight, his skin cold. He'd never had premonitions, but at that moment, he felt the way he had when the stranger in Armani had approached him, when he'd turned and seen the gun and known he was going to die. Liz wasn't going to kill him—not in public when she'd had plenty of time alone with him—but he suspected it was going to hurt like hell just the same.

She ended her call and started toward him. The pay phone rang when she was twenty feet away. He looked at it, looked back at her, then picked it up on the third ring. His hand was unsteady. So was his voice. "Yeah, this is Joe."

"It really is you," Josh said. "What's up? Is it Mom? Dad? Is something wrong—"

"They're okay." Joe watched Liz, stopped in her tracks.

"Thank God."

An odd phrase coming from Josh. He never worried about anyone but himself.

"I figure I'm the last person you'd want to talk to about anything concerning yourself, so what's up?"

Joe's reasons for calling now seemed pointless. To warn Josh? His brother knew people wanted him dead. To ask about

Liz? To find out if he was nothing more to her than a substitute for his brother?

To find out. Why she had come to Copper Lake. Why she had followed him today. Anything. Everything.

Grimly he turned his back to her. In the reflective glass that encircled the alcove, he could see her, not hesitant, not uncertain, but simply waiting. Watching.

"Tell me what you know about Liz Dalton."

There was a moment of silence, then Josh blew out his breath. "Jeez, I should have known she wouldn't give up, not when I left her handcuffed to the bed. Has she been bugging you? Is she bothering Mom and Dad, too?"

"Not that I know of. She said—" Joe's brain caught up with his brother's words. "You left your girlfriend handcuffed to a bed?"

Josh laughed, but there was more scorn to it than humor. "I know we put on a pretty good act, but *come on.* You know my type, and Liz ain't it. For one thing, she's got that whole right-and-wrong, law-and-order thing going on. For another, her IQ is *way* higher than her bra size, and for another, can you really imagine me—your brother, Josh—introducing her to my buddies—'Hey, guys, meet my girlfriend, Liz. She's a deputy U.S. marshal.' No freakin' way."

The rushing in Joe's ears gave Josh's next words a distant, hollow quality. "And by the way, her name isn't Dalton. It's Dillon. Marshal Dillon. From the old TV show. Get it?"

Joe got it.

All of it.

Chapter 10

Liz had just been outed. She could tell by the way Joe went stiff, could feel it in the chill radiating across the distance that separated them. He knew she was a fed. Knew that every single thing she'd said or done since the moment they'd met had been a lie.

Her muscles were knotted, holding her in place. She couldn't move closer as she should, couldn't grab the phone and demand that Josh turn himself in—for it had to be Josh. Who else would Joe call only from a pay phone?

She couldn't do a damn thing but stand there and regret.

She'd known it was going to be a tough day. She should have stayed in bed.

Hell, she should have stayed in Dallas.

His call was short, less than five minutes. He returned the receiver to the cradle, leaving his hand on it for a moment, before stepping away, then walking out the door.

Finally she could move. She jogged to the door and outside, and caught up with him fifty feet away before matching her pace to his. "Joe, we should talk."

He acted as if he didn't hear her.

"Joe." She laid her hand on his arm, and he jerked away as if her touch had seared him. He came to a stop so abruptly that she had to backtrack a few steps to face him.

"Talk?" he repeated softly. "What do you want to talk about, Marshal Dillon?"

She winced at the venom he put into her title and name. "I know you're angry—"

"Why should I be angry?" The emotion came off him in waves, heavy, relentless, suffocating. "You lied to me about your name, about your job, about your connection to Josh. You came to this town, you lied to Miss Abigail and Natalia and everyone else. You spied on me. You slept with me. And you think I might be *angry?*"

He wasn't yelling or gesturing or doing anything that might make a passerby think he was upset. He stood, loose-limbed, his expression blank, and his voice was pitched low and smooth. By all appearances, he was a normal man on a normal day having a normal conversation.

"I won't apologize for the lies," she said flatly, though someplace inside she was aching to do just that. "I was assigned to Josh's protection team undercover. The U.S. Attorney didn't want the Mulroneys to figure out the identity of the witness against them. I had no choice, for Josh's safety."

A muscle twitched in Joe's jaw, and his skin paled a shade. "So you kept Josh safe. You just let me get shot."

She flinched again. She had blamed the shooter, the Mulroneys and Josh—everyone but herself—but Joe was right. They should have been prepared for a murder attempt, however unlikely it seemed. They should have taken precautions to protect Josh's family, especially the brother who looked just like him. She, her team and her agency had nearly cost Joe his life.

Oh, God.

She drew a shallow breath. "I am sorry about that. We didn't know… We didn't think… We screwed up, Joe, and I'm damn sorry."

"Just not enough to be honest for once."

His scorn rankled, especially considering that she wasn't the only one who'd lied. "What if I'd been honest, Joe? What if I'd walked into your shop last week and said, 'Hi, you know me as Liz Dalton, Josh's girlfriend, but in reality, I'm Deputy Marshal Liz Dillon, and I'm trying to find your brother because he escaped custody'? Would you have said, 'Hey, yeah, I have a phone number for him'? Or would you have lied the way you lied to Tom Smith and to Deputy Marshal Ashe and to Daniel Wallace?"

Color crept into his face, and heat shaded his voice. "That's the *only* thing I lied to you about."

"Considering this is a criminal case, that's a pretty damn big lie."

"So arrest me."

"If we didn't have the information we need, I probably would." She watched his eyes widen, then narrow again. "As soon as I saw you on the phone, I called my supervisor. By the time you finished leaving your message, we had the number you dialed, and the instant Josh called back, we had his location pinpointed to within 75 feet. The Boulder police were setting up a perimeter before you hung up."

"You think I didn't figure that out? You think Josh didn't? He was moving while we talked. By the time we hung up, he was gone."

"Which makes you an accomplice in his escape."

Scowling, he dragged his fingers through his hair, leaving it on end. Liz sympathized with him more than she could say. All he'd wanted was to stay out of his brother's mess, but he'd wound up right in the middle of it. Again. Josh's fault. And hers.

When he finally spoke, his tone was quiet and bitter. "So, you got what you wanted, and it didn't even take much. A little deception, a little dishonesty, a little sex. Now you can get the hell away from me and, please, God, never come back."

He started walking then, long strides, around the corner and toward the front entrance of the mall. She matched him pace for pace. "Last night wasn't about the job, and you know it."

"Why? Because you say so? Hell, Liz, you wouldn't know the truth if it bit you on the ass." He directed a sardonic glare her way. "You do go by Liz, don't you? Or is it Beth or Elizabeth or Sandra or Jane?"

She quick-stepped to reach the bike before him, blocking his access to it. "Last night was about you and me and wanting what we'd believed for two years we couldn't have." He might deny it now, but he *had* wanted it, wanted her. She was positive of that. "It had nothing to do with work. Jeez, I could lose my job for it."

Her own words stopped her cold. Although it wasn't likely, she *could* lose her job. A few years ago, even a few weeks ago, that would have been unthinkable. All she'd ever wanted to be was a marshal. It had been the number one priority in her life. She couldn't have imagined *not* being a marshal.

But now she could. Now there were things she wanted more. To be a lover. A wife. A mother. To live a small-town life without weapons and badges. To stay in the same place year after year. To make friends without having to leave them behind with the next case or the next transfer.

And she wanted—oh, God, how she wanted—to see if she

could have that life with Joe. Just a chance. Was that too much to ask?

Judging by the scorn with which he regarded her, apparently so.

"Don't worry. I sure as hell won't tell anyone. It'll be our dirty little secret." He gripped her shoulders and firmly moved her out of the way, then unchained the bike. "Pack your stuff and get out. I'll say your goodbyes to Miss Abigail and Natalia."

Every nerve in Liz was quivering as she folded her arms across her middle. She couldn't force him to stay and listen to her. Well, actually, she could make him stay; he might be bigger and stronger, but she knew moves he didn't. But he couldn't hear words that he was too angry and hurt to acknowledge. Later, maybe. Once Josh had been taken into custody, once the initial surprise and the sense of betrayal had passed, once Joe was his reasonable, logical self again, she could explain.

Or maybe he would never be reasonable and logical again where she was concerned.

Without another glance her way, he climbed onto the bike and pedaled away. She stood where she was, ignoring the customers arriving and departing, ignoring for a time the ringing of her cell phone. It stopped after four rings, then immediately began again. She reached into her pocket and muted it, then pulled her keys from her other pocket. She waited for a car to pass, then stepped off the curb.

She'd grabbed the first parking space she found, near the end of the row directly in front of the entrance. There'd been a soccer-mom van in front of her and a candy-apple red Mustang beside her. Both cars were still there, along with a white panel van on the far side.

She would go home, she decided, and try to talk to Joe

again. When he refused to listen, she would call Mika; no doubt, that was who had just called her. Then she would… She would… There had to be something she would do, and curling up in bed for a good cry wouldn't be it. She wasn't a cryer. Growing up with three brothers had made sure of that. The stinging in her eyes was just from the sun or the humidity, and the lump in her throat just meant it was dry.

But her brothers had never had their hearts broken before, and at that moment, hers felt as if it would never mend.

She was thirty feet from her car when she realized that, next to it, the van's engine was running. There were no side windows in the back, and the front passenger windows were so heavily tinted she couldn't tell if it was occupied. There were no markings on the sides either. It was a completely non-descript van, the sort people would look at and forget entirely a minute later.

Goose bumps raised up her spine, and she slowed her steps for a quick scan of the area. It was one of those lulls in mall traffic where the parking lot was pretty much empty of people, and yet… Footsteps, slow and measured, sounded behind her. Sliding her cell phone from her pocket, unfastening the flap of her purse so her pistol was in easy gripping range, she made an abrupt turn at a hot orange Bug, crossed to the next aisle and cut back toward the stores.

Daniel Wallace stepped out from the cover of an SUV to block her way. "Forget something, Ms. Dalton?" he asked silkily.

A plan: Pretend she didn't know who he was and try to bluff her way past him? If there were people around, that might work; she might get close enough or make enough of a stir to draw attention her way. But he was big; he was fast; like her, he was almost certainly armed; and he wasn't alone. Someone was waiting for him in that van.

Liz edged to her right, putting the dinged-up rear end of a primer-coated Chevy between them. "What do you want?"

"You know the answer to that. I'm sure that in addition to warning the young girl who works at the coffee shop, Mr. Saldana warned you about me as well."

He'd called her Dalton, so he likely wasn't aware of her true identity; he would, like most men, underestimate her. He wouldn't want to give her a chance to cause a scene—someone could drive into the lot or come out of the mall at any moment—but he wouldn't expect her to put up a real fight. Grimly, she remembered her oldest brother's mantra from his high school sports days: *Ain't going down without a fight.*

Behind her the van's engine revved, underscored by the slow, rhythmic rub of tire on pavement. The driver had pulled out of the parking space and was approaching at a snail's crawl. She eased the GLOCK free of her bag, holding it loosely, comfortably, out of Wallace's range of vision. "If I knew where Josh was, I'd be there instead of here."

"If I believed you, I'd be in Chicago instead of Copper Lake."

She edged a few inches to her right. "Feel free to leave anytime."

His smile would have been charming if he wasn't so dangerous. "We think you and/or Mr. Saldana know how to contact the errant Josh. We think if he's not already in the area, it will take just a small amount of persuasion to bring him here."

"Me?" She managed a decent chuckle. "News flash. Josh and I aren't together anymore. He wouldn't cross the street to talk me. He damn sure isn't going to risk his life for me."

Wallace merely continued to smile.

"Come on, this is the guy who didn't stick around to see if his twin brother who got shot in his place was going to survive. Even if I had a way to get hold of him, he wouldn't come."

"You sell yourself short, Ms. Dalton. Ignoring his brother…"

He shrugged dismissively. "Ignoring the beautiful woman who shared his bed for more than two years…that's an entirely different matter."

Liz scanned the lot again. A car turned in off the street, then drove past to the other side of the mall. An elderly woman came out the main entrance, cane in hand, and started toward a Cadillac in the handicapped spaces. There were no familiar faces, no police cars, no gangs of brawny teenage boys who would consider it fun rescuing a woman in distress.

The van was now about twenty feet away. Had they expected her to go quietly? Was she supposed to be intimidated enough by Wallace that he could just shove her inside? Yeah, right. Flipping the phone open, she blindly dialed 911, took a breath, then lunged to the right, getting her feet under her, interrupting the operator before she could ask, *What's your emergency?* "Copper Lake Mall," she shouted into the phone, not daring to look back at the sound of squealing tires, not willing to estimate the distance separating Wallace's heavy tread from her. "I'm being kidnapped!"

Grateful for the thick-soled sandals she'd chosen in anticipation of a bike ride, she ran fast, hard, zigzagging around parked cars toward the entrance. They slowed her some, but with the benefit that they also slowed Wallace. She was halfway to the entrance, gaining ground, sirens sounding in the distance and racing closer. *Please let them be in time,* she prayed as she circled behind a monster SUV.

She caught the hint of movement an instant too late: a bare arm, tattooed beneath the short sleeve, muscular, hand clenched into a fist. She tried to swerve, tried to slow, but momentum pushed her forward, carrying her to meet the fist with its own momentum. The pain was instantaneous, nauseating. Her eyes filled with tears, her vision went blurry, her legs crumpled beneath her, and she fell, everything disappearing into blessed darkness.

Joe had never done any long-distance riding, but he found out that afternoon he could do nearly forty miles, the round-trip distance between Copper Lake and the next town to the east. His calf muscles were fatigued and burning by the time he pedaled back into town, but he was no more tired than when he'd ridden out of the mall. Not tired, hungry, angry. Just numb. Physically, emotionally, mentally. He wanted to stay that way for a damn long time.

He'd passed the mall, refusing to look at the square building or the parking lot even in his peripheral vision. He kept his gaze narrowly focused on the pavement ahead of him, maintaining a safe, constant distance between his front wheel and the curb, so focused that when a car going the opposite direction spun around, tires squealing, and blocked both westbound lanes, he managed to stop only an inch from the vehicle's rear quarter panel.

A. J. Decker jumped out of the car. "Where the hell have you been? We've been looking for you for hours." With the efficiency of the longtime cop he was, he located Joe's cell in his pocket—turned off—and swore. "These things aren't worth crap unless you turn 'em on."

Joe glared at him. "If I turn it on, people call."

Decker turned it on, waited for it to boot up, then shoved it in Joe's face. "You think?" he asked sarcastically.

The screen showed thirty-eight missed calls. Jeez, and he'd been gone only three hours. He took the phone and started to check the numbers, but Decker snatched it back, closing it. "They're probably all from us."

In that instant, the numbness disappeared. Hands shaking, Joe removed his helmet, fastened the chin strap and dangled it from the handle bars. "Josh," he murmured. The Boulder police had found him, and, being Josh, he'd done something stupid. Was he hurt? Dead? Oh, man, if his brother was dead because Joe had wanted to know if it was okay for him to have slept with Liz…

"When's the last time you saw Liz?" Decker asked.

Joe blinked. "A few hours ago. A little after twelve. Why?" Had she gotten the word from her supervisor? Had she asked Decker to break the news because she knew he'd rather not see her again as long as he lived?

"Where?"

"At the mall." Joe asked again, "Why?"

Decker's expression was grim. "Apparently she's been kidnapped."

Kidnapped. The word didn't compute. Not Liz. After he left, she would have gotten in her car and gone home. She would have checked in with her supervisor and, if there was a God in heaven, she would have packed up and left town. After all, she'd gotten what she wanted; she'd said as much. There was no reason for her to stick around. Not him. Certainly not their phony little affair.

"She's not kidnapped. She's just gone."

Decker's expression didn't lighten. "911 got a call from a woman screaming that she was being kidnapped at the mall. We found Liz's car parked in the lot. Her cell phone was on the ground behind another vehicle, and there was blood, both on the phone and splattered on the ground around it. What we can't find is Liz. You have any idea why?"

The people and events of the last few days flashed through Joe's mind with such intensity that his head hurt: Liz, Tom Smith, Ashe, Wallace, the near hit-and-run, the sex last night, finding out the truth today. There was little chance Smith or Ashe would have taken her; they were feds, too.

They knew her; she knew them; she would have gone with them willingly.

Wallace? He'd tried to buy Josh's location from Joe and failed. Was he capable of kidnapping Liz? Of course he was.

Was he willing to kill her?

He shied away from the question, from even the possibility that Liz was in Wallace's, and therefore the Mulroneys', hands. This was just another of her deceptions. Maybe the cops hadn't been able to catch Josh in Boulder; maybe they thought if they pretended that Liz had been kidnapped, that her life was in danger, Joe would tell them something more. Not that he had anything left to tell, but why would they believe that when he'd lied to them all along?

But if it was real… His gut tightened. If it was real, would he trade Josh for Liz?

No matter how angry she'd made him or how badly she'd hurt him, there was only one answer. Not only yes, but hell, yes. Falling for her might qualify as the stupidest thing he'd ever done, but mistake or not, he'd be damned if he would let anything happen to her. He wanted her gone, out of his memory and out of his life, but not dead. Never dead.

"Joe?" Decker prodded. "Why would someone kidnap Liz Dalton?"

His head throbbed; his stomach churned. He could barely make his mouth move. "Because they think she knows where my brother is. They think she'll tell them or…or I will."

"Who are they? Why do they want your brother? Where is he?"

Sickly, Joe met his gaze. "A few hours ago, he was in Colorado. Boulder. Now…" He shrugged. Now it was anyone's guess. Josh could have gone to ground in Boulder, hidden so well that not even a pack of bloodhounds could find him, or he could be well on his way elsewhere.

Decker stared back for a minute, then opened the trunk of the car. "Put your bike in here." Together they heaved it in, though the trunk lid wouldn't close. Joe slid into the passenger seat, remembering to fasten the belt only when the reminder dinged.

As Decker pulled back into traffic, he said, "I'm guessing you've got a long story to tell. First, though, check those missed calls. See if any of them *aren't* from the cops."

It was the seventh call, an out-of-area number. He punched the buttons to get to the corresponding voice mail, then switched to speaker phone as the message began. "Mr. Saldana, it's Daniel Wallace. Since you weren't receptive to my offer last night, I've raised the stakes a bit. I've got Ms. Dalton, but I'll happily return her unharmed—more or less—in exchange for your brother. I'll be in touch with you soon with the details."

Something inside Joe died: the faint hope that this was another of Liz's lies. The feds, he'd discovered—Liz, he reminded himself; she was a fed, too—weren't above making complete fools of innocent people to achieve their goals, but they wouldn't use the Mulroneys' people to do it.

He would return her unharmed, Wallace had said. *More or less.* Joe's gut clenched again, his fingers whitening around the phone. They'd found blood along with her phone. What had the bastard done to her? Obviously she hadn't gone with him willingly, or she wouldn't have called 911. Had he merely subdued her? Or worse? How much worse?

"Any other calls from him?" Decker asked as he turned into the police department parking lot.

Startled by the cop's voice, Joe refocused on the missed-calls screen, then shook his head. Every other call had come from the police department, Decker or Tommy Maricci.

Decker's next question didn't come until they were seated in a conference room inside the department with Maricci, Pete Petrovski and KiKi Isaacs, Copper Lake's lone female detective. "Why don't you start at the beginning? Tell us everything you know about Liz, your brother and Daniel Wallace."

"I will. But one thing you need to know up front… Liz's name isn't Dalton. It's Dillon, and she's a U.S. marshal."

Decker and Maricci exchanged looks, muttering the same curse at the same time, and Maricci rose from the table. "I'll call Atlanta."

"Ask for a marshal named Ashe. He's familiar with the case." Joe took a deep breath, then slowly blew it out. He'd lived in this town a while. He considered these people friends, and they thought the same of him. They were about to find out just how much he'd hidden from them.

"I have a brother, an identical twin. We lived in Chicago, and two years ago…"

They let him talk without interruption, and he told them everything. Except about the night before. Except the personal parts of his conversation with Liz at the mall. Damn it, if he hadn't been so pissed off, if he'd done the reasonable thing and gone home with her to talk it out… If he'd at least offered the courtesy of walking her to her car…

But he hadn't had any courtesy inside him after finding out that while he'd fallen in love with her, he was nothing more to her than a pawn in the government's game to get Josh. All the lies, all the hurt—he'd just wanted to run away.

And while he was embracing Josh's childish tendency to flee, Wallace was forcing Liz into his vehicle, taking her hostage to use as his own pawn. Threatening her, scaring her, making her bleed.

Joe had never felt such impotent rage, not when he'd awakened in the hospital with red-hot pain consuming him. Not even when he'd found out it was because of Josh.

"So you don't know if the cops found your brother in

Colorado," Decker said. When Joe shook his head, his expression tightened. "It's not like we can just call the Boulder PD and ask, not with this being a federal case. Do you still have the number?"

Joe pulled the crumpled paper from his pocket. It was damp with sweat from his long ride, the ink smudged, but the digits were legible. Decker dialed the number from the landline on the table between them, then handed the receiver to Joe. This time the call went straight to voice mail. "It's me. Joe. Call me as soon as you can. It's urgent." He read off the number from the phone, listened until the cell clicked off, then slowly hung up.

"If his calls are going straight to voice mail either he's on another call or the cell's shut off," Maricci remarked. "I doubt he's got much of a social life, being on the run. But with the cell turned off, the feds can't use its GPS to track him."

"We can assume they didn't catch him in Boulder," Decker added, "or a cop would have answered that call."

Maricci leaned back in his chair. "So Wallace and at least one accomplice have Liz, and they want to trade her for your brother's whereabouts—"

"If we're lucky," Decker interjected.

"Or for your brother himself. We can give him a location, but he's not gonna let Liz go until his people have Josh in custody, and because you don't know where he is, that's not gonna happen."

At the end of the table, KiKi spoke up. "I have a suggestion. Let's write up a report and go home. This is a federal case. The FBI and the marshals service are going to come swooping in here within the hour and take over. All they'll want from us is coffee and doughnuts, so let's not waste our time."

Petrovski rolled his eyes, and Maricci scowled. Decker directed a cool gaze her way. "Never miss an opportunity to keep your mouth shut and learn," he said in a level voice.

Bright spots of color appeared in KiKi's cheeks as he went on. "She's right about one thing. I imagine we'll have fifteen to twenty feds here soon, and we'll be pretty much out of the loop in their investigation. But that doesn't mean we just blow it off."

"Maybe Wallace will call before they get here," Joe said.

"And you'll give him what?"

He smiled thinly. "Josh."

"You said he was in Colorado."

"He is. Was. But Wallace doesn't know that for a fact."

The room was quiet for a moment, everyone watching him. Did they think he was nuts? He wouldn't argue. Reckless? Out of his freakin' mind?

Decker rubbed his hand over the beard stubble on his jaw. "Do you know how dangerous that would be?"

"Did I mention that Josh and I are identical? Give us the same haircut and put us in the same clothes, and even our parents can't tell us apart. Wallace wouldn't know the difference." Except for the scars. He might pick up on those.

"Maybe not, but have you thought ahead to *after* the trade?" Petrovski asked. "After Liz is gone and you're still there? They want to kill your brother, which means they would want to kill *you*."

Joe swallowed hard. He'd never been an adrenaline junkie like Josh. He'd come close to dying once and he didn't want to do it again, not until he was at least ninety. But letting them kill Liz was unthinkable. Better that he take his chances with Wallace than her.

"We'd rather get her back without sacrificing you," Decker said, then smiled one of his rare smiles. "But it's a plan."

He didn't say what kind of plan. He didn't need to. One doomed to disaster. But what other choice did they have? Either Liz's life was on the line, or his was, and he couldn't live if it was hers.

While the cops talked, he leaned his head back and closed his eyes. Now he was tired, though not from the bike ride or the restless night. All he'd wanted from Copper Lake was peace and security, and he'd had it for two years. Then Liz had come, and those damn dogs and everyone else, and peace and security had disappeared out the window. He wanted it back.

He wanted *her* back.

Restlessly, he picked up his cell and dialed Natalia's number. It went to voice mail. "Hey, Nat, it's Joe. I'm not gonna be home for a while, so can you let Bear and Elizabeth out now, then feed them supper around seven? Thanks."

"You named your dog after your girlfriend?" Maricci asked with a grin.

"You'd be surprised how much they have in common."

KiKi snorted. "I'm surprised she didn't shoot you between the eyes."

"She took it as a compliment." He smiled faintly at the memory. Liz had been wearing a short dress and amazingly sexy heels and drinking a frozen coffee. Watching her lick the whipped cream off the straw had left him so weak in the knees that if he hadn't been sitting, he would have fallen at her feet.

Pain slashed, sharp and lethal, through him.

"We'll get her back," Maricci said quietly.

It was a guess, no better than Joe's best guess—or his worst—but he grabbed the hope it offered.

Then his cell phone rang. His fingers spasmed as he reached for it, turning on the speaker, and the rushing in his ears nearly blocked out Decker's quiet admonition. *Stay calm.*

Daniel Wallace sounded as cool and in control as ever. "Mr. Saldana, ask one of those police officers with you for his cell phone number. I want to send you a video."

Decker gave his number, and a moment later his phone beeped.

"We want your brother, Mr. Saldana," Wallace said.

Joe's response was automatic. "I don't know where he is."

"Then that's very unfortunate for Ms. Dalton, because you have only until midnight tonight to gain her release. Ask the officer to show you the video."

Decker held out his phone, and everyone gathered to watch over Joe's shoulder. The room on the small screen was dark except for the light shining on Liz's face. Her cheek was scraped raw, her left eye swollen shut, her nose and upper lip puffy and dried blood trailed across her skin. She lay motionless, eyes closed, lips slightly parted. She could be unconscious. She could be dead.

Then, after a mumbled command, a booted foot came into frame, nudging her shoulder. Her lashes fluttered, her forehead wrinkled and a low moan escaped her.

And the clip ended.

Tension expanded in Joe's chest, making it damn near impossible to breathe. "How am I supposed to find Josh and have him here by midnight?"

"That's not my problem, Mr. Saldana."

"I need more time."

"Sorry." Wallace sounded professional, strictly business. "I operate on the schedule I'm given. Midnight. I'll call you again to tell you where we'll make the exchange. Just you and your brother. No one else."

Wallace hung up, and Joe did the same, his hand shaking. Across the table, Decker and Maricci were watching the video once more. He didn't ask to see it again. The image of Liz's battered face was burned into his brain.

Please, God, don't let it be the last picture I have of her.

It took every bit of strength Liz possessed to open her eyes. Her lids felt heavy and her vision was fuzzy, limited on the left. Her shoulders ached, and her wrists…movement showed they were secured together behind her back with what felt like thick cable ties. Her entire face throbbed, especially around her left eye, which was tender, swollen, probably spectacularly black. Her cheekbones hurt, the inside of her mouth was sore and the taste of blood lingered on her tongue.

She hoped the jerk who had hit her had at least a few scrapes to show for it.

She was inside the van, lying on her side, and her head was pounding—from the blow? From being unconscious so long? The sky visible through the van's windshield was black, dimly broken by distant stars. A long time to stay knocked out from a simple blow. Although, she thought dizzily as she started the painful process of sitting up without the help of her hands, there had been nothing simple about that blow.

Finally semi-vertical, she sagged against the van wall as voices sounded outside, three, distinct, although their words were little more than murmurs. One was Daniel Wallace, politely menacing. One seemed vaguely familiar, nothing definite that she could point to, just the feeling that she knew it. The other was a stranger.

Wallace's voice grew louder as he came nearer the van. An instant after his words stopped, the back door opened, and he appeared, handsome, elegant, dangerous in the dim overhead light. "Our guest is finally awake. I admit, I was starting to wonder if my associate miscalculated the dosage of the sedative he gave you."

She looked past him, but both of his associates were hidden from view. All she could see was heavy woods and, to the left, faint light reflected on water. Copper Lake? That was where Joe was supposed to have taken her this afternoon, on Natalia's borrowed bike. She would much prefer his company to Wallace's.

Wallace moved to sit in the open door. "You've slept half the day away, Liz. You don't mind if I call you that, do you? Ms. Dalton seems so formal, given the circumstances."

"By all means, Danny, go ahead." Her voice was hoarse, her throat dry.

His gaze narrowed before he treated her to the predatory smile again. "I'm sorry about your injuries. If you'd just come along nicely, there would have been no need for violence."

No need? He intended to kill her. No doubt he'd called Joe, offering to trade her for Josh, but even if Joe could pull that off, Wallace still had to kill her. He and his buddies had kidnapped her, assaulted her and were holding her hostage—all felonies. How much easier to add murder to their list than to leave a victim alive and able to identify them.

They would kill Joe, too.

She didn't want to die, didn't want him to die, especially thinking so little of her. If she'd just tried harder to explain things to him, if she'd just been more honest about her feelings for him.... She'd told him she'd wanted him. Wanted. Not *needed*. Not *loved*.

The cuts inside her mouth hurt when she smiled, but she forced the action. "Gee, I never have been the type to play well with others."

"I thought I knew your type—Saldana's type. All flash, no substance. Empty-headed, neither bright nor capable, willing to do whatever it takes to catch and hold on to a guy. And yet inside that cute little purse, along with your lipstick, money and debit card, you had a GLOCK .45. That's a hell of a gun for a pretty woman like you. Why do you carry it?"

"Because of scum like you." He waited for more, and she went on after a moment. "You know the kind of people Josh gets mixed up with. Better safe than sorry."

"I bet right now you're sorry you didn't shoot me in the parking lot."

She smiled. "There's still time."

He glanced at his watch. "Not much. I gave Saldana a deadline of midnight. It's ten till. Either he delivers his brother or…" An eloquent shrug that said so much. Or they would kill her and Joe both, and when Josh found out, he would go into hiding for the rest of his life. The Mulroneys would never have to worry about him again.

"Come on," Wallace said, rising, dusting his pants. "Let's get you out of there."

Shrinking away from the hand he offered, she scooted to the open door, lowered her feet to the ground and gingerly stood up, then followed him to the front of the van. They were in a clearing at the lake's edge, parked next to a picnic pavilion. On the other side were two other vehicles: a black SUV—gee, no surprise there—and, barely visible beyond that, the front end of a compact car. Wallace's accomplices were standing in the shadow of the pavilion, two dark figures, one tall and stout, the other shorter and thinner. Stout held a rifle and faced the road. Short held a pistol at his side and faced the lake.

A ripping sound brought her attention back to Wallace. He'd torn a six-inch strip off a roll of duct tape and was coming toward her, smiling. He pressed it across her mouth, gently smoothing the edges, then gestured to the west. "Walk out there to the middle of the field and sit down."

Liz gauged the distance to the center: thirty feet, tops. If she made a break for the woods on either side, a halfway decent shot with a halfway decent rifle would bring her down. She started walking across grass that had recently had its first cut since winter and smelled sweetly of straw, summer and lazy days.

Before she'd gone fifteen feet, she became aware of an engine in the distance, and her heart seized in her chest. *Joe.*

A set of headlights came on, followed by two more, elongating her shadow at odd angles. If she turned back to face them, she would be blinded. Joe would be blinded, too, dealing with disembodied voices, unable to see their weapons.

"That's far enough," Wallace called, and she stopped. "Sit down."

She did that, too, awkwardly, settling sideways so she could see both the road and the bad guys, as yet another set of headlights flashed briefly through the trees ahead. The SUV that came slowly around the bend was dark in color and belonged to Tommy Maricci; he'd given her and Joe a ride home in it just a few nights ago.

The headlights swept across her as the vehicle slowed even more, then turned off the road into the grass. It stopped, the engine still running, the headlights still on, but long moments dragged past before the door finally opened and the driver slid out.

Liz had to squint to see the still figure beyond. She wanted to scream at Joe to get back in the truck and race away, to demand of him why he'd taken so dangerous a risk, to apologize, to tell him she loved him.

Of course she couldn't tell him anything, so it was Wallace who broke the silence. "Turn off those lights and come closer. Show us which Saldana we've got."

Joe reached inside the truck, and the lights mercifully went dark. He closed the door with a thud and started across the field, so familiar and yet…not. The way he moved, the way he held his head, the smug self-assurance that radiated from him—to say nothing of the way he hardly even glanced at her…if she didn't know better, she would think he was Josh. But no way Josh was in Georgia, and no way he'd be out here offering to trade himself to the people who wanted him dead.

Nausea swept over her. It was Joe pretending to be Josh,

and he was just good enough at it to get himself killed. For her. *With* her. *Oh, God.*

"So?" Wallace prodded. "Which one are you?"

Joe stopped alongside her, maybe ten feet away, arms extended in a casual gesture. "Which one you think?" His clothes were different, all in black: jeans, a T-shirt a size too small so it fitted snugly, heavy boots and leather jacket. His voice was different, too, subtly, but in ways a perceptive person would notice.

"It's a shame," Wallace said, his own voice coming from behind the bright lights of the SUV and the car. "Identical twins can be so difficult to tell apart. It would be nice to think that Josh is man enough to take responsibility for himself and save his former girlfriend from death, but when has he ever taken responsibility? The odds of him coming here to rescue Liz are probably about nil. Joe, on the other hand, is the responsible brother. The one who would put his life on the line for the woman he loves. The one who would die in his brother's place so that she might live."

Liz tried to speak in spite of the tape, managing a few shrill sounds that only Joe heard.

He gave her an insolent look eerily like the looks Josh had given her countless times over the two years they were together, then he turned his attention back to the unseen Wallace. "Yeah, yeah, Joe's the responsible one, the good one. He never does anything wrong, and I never get anything right. I've heard it all before, trust me. But I figure I kind of owe him after your guy shot him instead of me, so here I am. You let her go, and we'll deal."

"Let her go," Wallace echoed. "You know it's not that simple. As you mentioned, the last time, our people shot Joe instead of Josh. This time we need to be sure."

Liz tried frantically to get Joe's attention again. The man

had just admitted to, at the least, conspiracy to commit murder in Joe's shooting. He wasn't planning on letting either of them walk away after that, but Joe could still save himself if he'd just look at her, if he would just think rationally.

"And how're you gonna be sure?"

"Fortunately, I've brought someone with me who knows both of you well. She can tell me who you are."

Liz looked at the confusion evident on Joe's face—who did he and Josh have in common these days besides her and their mother?—then twisted to watch as a figure emerged from the darkness of the pavilion. Long stride, graceful, familiar in her quiet wallflower way.

"Son of a…" Joe murmured as she came closer, separating enough from the brilliance of the lights that they could make out details. Short brown hair. Waifish. Eyes that changed color as easily as her mood. Pistol clasped in one hand as casually as if it were Bear's leash.

Dear God. *Natalia.*

"Natalia?" The rushing in Joe's ears was so loud that he wasn't sure he'd actually spoken her name. What was she doing here? Why was she with Wallace? How the hell did she know Josh?

Another liar. She'd come to town right after Josh escaped custody, feeding Joe sad stories, playing on his gullibility, earning his trust and his affection, and the whole time she was working for the Mulroneys.

His stomach heaved, and for a panicked instant, he thought he would puke out his guts there in front of everyone. But he swallowed hard, forcing down the fear, concentrating on the cops who were out there, unseen, doing their best to protect him and Liz.

"You lied," he muttered when Natalia drew close enough.

No use pretending with her. Like Liz, she knew him too well to fall for the act.

Her eyes were black tonight—mourning? he wondered sarcastically. Her pale face still looked about fifteen, still looked innocent, although her features seemed locked in an emotionless mask.

"You work for those guys?" He jerked his head toward Wallace but included everyone all the way back to Chicago.

"Sometimes." As she slid the pistol into the holster on her belt, she moved in a slow circle around him, looking him and up down in a measuring manner, as if she hadn't known he was Joe before she'd left the cover of darkness.

She circled him again, moving so close that their clothes rubbed, then she rose onto her toes and kissed him. Startled and disgusted, he jerked back, but she simply gripped the back of his neck with iron strength, rose and kissed him again, with her mouth, her tongue, with hunger.

Fury pounded through Joe with every beat of his heart, holding him rigid. He was hardly aware of her free hand fumbling at his waist, pulling at his shirt. When her fingers slid under the fabric and across his ribcage, he realized she was looking for the scars. She touched one, then the other, then slowly broke the kiss and turned to face Wallace.

"It's him. Josh."

Joe's anger drained as he stared at her. She'd lied. Again. The lie would get him killed for sure, but maybe it would give Liz a chance to escape.

"On your knees," Natalia ordered, and he numbly obeyed. A few feet away, she was pulling Liz to her feet, steadying her. She unfolded a wicked blade from her pocket and sliced through the plastic securing Liz's wrists, ripped away the duct tape from her mouth, then gave her a push toward the car.

"You're free to go, Ms. Dalton," Wallace called from his hiding place.

Liz stood where she was, battered, stunned, as if she hadn't heard the words. She started to rub one wrist, then looked down numbly at the raw, ragged skin. Even though her voice was little more than a whisper, Joe understood her easily. "Bastard."

"Get out of here, Liz," Joe said. It was too easy to imagine her arguing that she couldn't go, that deputy U.S. marshals didn't save themselves by leaving others to die.

She looked at him then, her injuries somehow worse in the faint light. "I am so sorry."

He smiled a little. "So am I."

"I don't suppose you left a weapon in the car."

He shook his head—his own lie. Decker had given him a gun. *I don't know how to use that,* Joe had said, and Decker had brushed him off. *Liz does.*

"I'm sorry," she murmured again as Natalia took her arm and began pushing her to the car. "I love you."

He grinned. "Don't you think last night would have been a better time to tell me that?" Then none of this would have happened, because they'd still be naked in the back office at the coffee shop.

"You know, you could have said it then, too."

He couldn't grin now, pardon the expression, to save his life. "I love you, Liz." First time he'd ever said those words.

Likely to be the last.

"Sweet," Natalia said as she hustled Liz toward the car.

"How could you—"

"Shut up and listen to me. Get in the car and drive back the way he came. There's a sign just after the curve. Go exactly one-tenth mile, and there's a trail that goes off the road on the left. It comes out at the lake's edge about twenty feet from the van. *Don't* go back to the main road. They've set up an ambush at the park entrance. Wallace has no intention of letting you leave here alive."

"And you do?" Liz asked skeptically.

Natalia smiled one of her rare smiles. "I have every intention of you *and* Joe getting out of here alive."

Liz wondered if Natalia was leading her into an ambush, not away from one. She'd trusted Natalia, Joe had trusted her, and she'd fooled them both. "How well do you know Josh?"

Natalia's smile faded into bittersweet pain. "I'd die for him."

"Yeah, people seem to have that feeling for him," Liz muttered with a glance at Joe.

"He wouldn't die for Josh," Natalia disagreed. "He's here for you. Remember—one-tenth mile, then left."

Liz climbed into the SUV, closed the door, then reached down to scoot the seat forward. Her fingers brushed cool metal, ridged, an object so familiar to her that she could recognize it blindfolded. She lifted the .45 into her lap, positioning it between her legs for easy gripping, then shifted into gear.

Driving away and leaving Joe behind was the hardest thing she'd ever done. Still on his knees, he watched her until the first curve blocked the view. "Oh, God," she whispered, the best prayer she could manage.

A hundred feet around the curve was a sign for a hiking trail. She alternately watched the odometer and the left side of the road for a break in the trees. When it appeared, she switched off the headlights, then turned onto the broad dirt path. She navigated by moonlight, driving slowly to keep engine noise to a minimum, easing to a stop where the trail crossed a footbridge over a creek that emptied into the lake.

Liz climbed out of the car, pushing the door until it closed with a quiet click. She had eleven shots in the pistol, and she wanted to put every one of them into Daniel Wallace, then find the GLOCK he'd taken from her and empty that magazine into him as well. If anything happened to Joe...

She crossed the bridge, then cut into the woods. The clearing came into sight after the first twenty yards, still well lit by the headlights, Joe still on his knees, Natalia nearby. Occasional snatches of conversation carried through the trees, but they were impossible to understand.

She was moving from the scant cover of one thin tree to another, working her way closer to both the clearing and the lake shore, when a hand slid over her mouth while another gripped her pistol hand tightly.

"It's Lieutenant Decker," he whispered in her ear.

She nodded to show she understood, and he let go, then moved to her side. "Maricci and Petrovski are in the trees to the north. How many besides the girl?"

"Two that I know of. Plus an ambush set up at the entrance."

Shielding his cell phone with one hand, Decker typed a quick text message, hit Send, then pocketed the device. "Isn't that the girl who lives next door to Saldana?"

Liz nodded. "She told Wallace he's Josh. She told me how to find the trail leading here and about the ambush."

"So maybe we shouldn't shoot her if we don't have to." Even in a raspy whisper, Decker's dry humor came through.

"I would prefer that we don't." There must be extenuating circumstances explaining why Natalia was working with Wallace. Liz and Joe were good judges of character, and she couldn't believe that they'd been so totally wrong about Natalia. It was almost surely Josh's fault somehow that she'd been dragged into this.

"How good a shot are you with this?" Decker lifted the scoped rifle slung over his shoulder. "Can you go back about thirty feet and take out some of those headlights?"

"You bet." She took the weapon, exchanged nods with him

and eased back the way she'd come. When she paused to look back, Decker was gone. No sign, no sound.

Wishing she was wearing black like everyone else, she located the biggest tree near the edge of the piney woods, an oak that was nothing like the massive ones she'd seen in town but that was at least wider than she was. Taking cover against the trunk, she sighted on the headlights one at a time, drew a breath to steady herself, then began picking them off.

Within forty seconds, the field went dark. Wallace began shouting out orders as gunfire erupted. Natalia grabbed Joe's arm, jerking him to his feet, and together they sprinted for the woods a few yards west of Liz.

"Run, run, run," she whispered as a burst of gunshots bit into the ground in their wake. Joe pulled free of Natalia, took her arm the same way she'd held his, and lengthened his stride, dragging her after him. When they reached the tree line, he dived to the ground, pulling her with him, then they scuttled to the nearest big tree for cover.

Over near the vehicles, there were a few last shots, then unnatural silence fell. After a moment, a shrill whistle pierced the night before Decker stepped out of the shadows. "It's clear. Come on out."

Liz slung the rifle strap over her shoulder and raced to the next oak, skidding to a stop on the other side. Natalia was sitting up, brushing dead leaves from her hair. Joe lay on his back, eyes closed, pale, motionless. For an instant, Liz's heart stopped beating, then he blew out a deep breath and looked up at her. "Damn, you're beautiful."

She dropped to her knees. "I can only guess how I look based on the way I feel, but I'm pretty sure only a crazy man could call it beautiful."

"Just crazy in love." He sat up, then touched her face so

lightly that she hardly felt it, her swollen lip, her bruised cheek, the corner of her black eye. "I hope Decker kicks him in the face, lets him see how it feels."

"Honey, Decker probably put a bullet in his brain," she said gently. Joe was such a good guy, not accustomed to the use of deadly force. She wouldn't let him blame himself for anything that had happened tonight.

"Even better." He got to his feet, helped her up, then wrapped his arms around her middle. "Don't get kidnapped again," he murmured, his lips brushing her temple.

"I'll try not to."

"Don't get shot at again." He kissed her ear.

"Okay."

"Don't scare me like that again." This time his mouth trailed along the right side of her jaw, making her shiver.

"I won't."

Then he bent so close that their noses bumped and stared fiercely into her eyes. "Don't break my heart, Liz."

Warmth swelled through her. He wanted her—not Liz Dalton, his brother's ex-girlfriend, but Deputy Marshal Liz Dillon. His *I love you* hadn't been an obligated response or a dying declaration that he'd never have to live up to. He wanted her. Loved her. Would be broken-hearted without her.

She threw her arms around his neck and hugged him tightly enough to make his breath catch. "Never," she whispered. "I'll never, ever break anything. I love you, Joe."

His kiss was gentle, awkward, a little bit painful and the sweetest kiss she'd ever had. She was vaguely aware through the haze that surrounded her of footsteps moving away, then Decker's distant voice.

"Are they okay back there?"

Then Natalia. "They're alive and together. Yeah. They're okay."

* * *

Liz dressed carefully Wednesday morning, choosing a sleeveless white dress that molded to her curves, with a red belt snug at her waist. It went well with Joe's favorite red-and-white heels, and her favorite red purse that fastened with a big leather bow. Her hair was loose around her shoulders, and her makeup was carefully applied to camouflage her injuries.

She looked pretty damn good, she thought as she stared at herself in the mirror. She needed the confidence of that because she was on a mission today.

Leaving her car where it was, she set out for a leisurely walk downtown for a not-so-leisurely talk with Joe. Things were good between them, just unsettled. Since Sunday night, they'd made love, talked, made love some more, but they hadn't discussed the future. They'd each said *I love you,* but they hadn't talked about what that meant. She knew what it meant to her: commitment, marriage, kids, the rest of their lives. She needed to know what it meant to him.

A lot of other things had been settled since Sunday. Daniel Wallace had been wounded and arrested and faced a laundry list of charges. Being an intelligent man, he would probably put his best interests first and testify against his employers. His associate at the clearing was dead, and the four men who had set up the ambush for Liz were all in custody.

Josh *wasn't* in custody. His phone had eventually been located at a Boulder mall, in the possession of a twelve-year-old boy who'd found it in a McDonald's. No one had a clue where to look for him now.

Natalia wasn't in custody either. She'd been taken back to the police station with the other survivors, had answered a few questions, asked to go to the bathroom and quietly disappeared. The feds had been furious, but Decker and Maricci—who'd never lost a prisoner in their lives—weren't fazed by it.

Liz would have let her go, too.

She stopped at an intersection and realized that she'd reached the square while her thoughts had wandered. A Cuppa Joe was across the street, the tables mostly empty. She drew a breath for courage, crossed the street and went inside.

Joe came out of the back room, grinning when he saw her. His gaze dropped to her feet and made a long, slow trip back up, and arousal entered his expression. "Hey," he greeted her. "It's a slow morning, you look incredibly hot, and I've got a couch in the back. What do you say?"

She gave him a chastising look. "Is it slow enough that we can talk?"

His smile faded, and disquiet entered his expression. She empathized. If he'd told her, *We need to talk*, her palms would be clammy and the edges of her heart would already be breaking in anticipation of the bad news to come.

"Sure," he said. "Come on back."

When she went into the office, she noticed a box on his desk, the lid askew and showing a bit of porcelain. More coffee mugs. Probably recycled or handmade in some tiny start-up third-world pottery. He did like saving his corner of the earth.

He stopped in the doorway, facing her. "What's up?"

Jeez, it was easier to think about asking him what he wanted than to actually do it. What if he wanted a long-distance affair? What if he didn't want her in his life on a daily basis? After all, she must come with some pretty bad memories attached.

"I, uh, I'm supposed to be back in Dallas next week, and, uh, I was wondering…"

His face went blank of all expression as his body went stiff.

She took a breath and rushed on. "I was wondering what you thought about that. Whether you mind. Whether you want or don't want me to stay here, at least all the time, because I could understand if you didn't, but—"

She broke off when he abruptly moved, striding to the desk and lifting the lid from the box. He thrust it at her, and she stared at the tall, gracefully shaped cup inside. A whimsical view of Copper Lake beneath a summer blue sky circled the cup—A Cuppa Joe, the square, River's Edge, Wyndham Hall, SnoCap. And in the place of prominence, a house: white, dark shutters, picket fence, flowers blooming everywhere, and a mailbox on a crooked post. Tiny print on the mailbox read *Liz and Joe.* And even tinier, under that, *Forever.*

She clasped the mug in both hands, tears filling her eyes. "Oh, Joe…"

He set the box aside, then wrapped his arms around her. "I love you, Liz. I want to marry you. I want to have kids with you. I won't ask you to quit your job or move here. I can go—"

She smiled up at him. "Oh, please do. Really. Please ask." Giving him the precious cup to hold, she reached inside her purse and drew out a single sheet of paper.

It was a letter she'd never imagined herself writing. Until lately, it had been unthinkable, even, but when she'd started to write, the words had come easily. Joe was definitely one of the reasons, but there were others. Finding a life she wanted more. Getting kidnapped. Facing death. Facing *his* death. Life was too short to spend one more day doing something that didn't own her heart.

"What's that?" he asked as she unfolded it.

"My resignation from the marshals service. Please ask me to stay, Joe."

He scanned the letter she held and the tension faded from his gaze. Staring down at her, he obeyed beautifully. "Will you marry me, Liz, and stay in Copper Lake?"

He was a good man, handsome as hell, sexy, dependable, and he'd proven himself willing to die for her. And she loved him. How could she possibly leave him?

"I will," she whispered. "Forever."

* * * * *

*Fan favorite Leslie Kelly is bringing her readers
a fantasy so scandalous,
we're calling it FORBIDDEN!*

*Look for
PLAY WITH ME
Available February 2010 from Harlequin® Blaze™.*

"Aren't you going to say 'Fly me' or at least 'Welcome Aboard'?"

Amanda Bauer didn't. The softly muttered word that actually came out of her mouth was a lot less welcoming. And had fewer letters. Four, to be exact.

The man shook his head and tsked. "Not exactly the friendly skies. Haven't caught the spirit yet this morning?"

"Make one more airline-slogan crack and you'll be walking to Chicago," she said.

He nodded once, then pushed his sunglasses onto the top of his tousled hair. The move revealed blue eyes that matched the sky above. And yeah. They were twinkling. Damn it.

"Understood. Just, uh, promise me you'll say 'Coffee, tea or me' at least once, okay? Please?"

Amanda tried to glare, but that twinkle sucked the annoyance right out of her. She could only draw in a slow breath as he climbed into the plane. As she watched her passenger disappear into the small jet, she had to wonder about the trip she was about to take.

Coffee and tea they had, and he was welcome to them. But her? Well, she'd never even considered making a move on a customer before. Talk about unprofessional.

And yet…

Something inside her suddenly wanted to take a chance, to be a little outrageous.

How long since she had done indecent things—or decent ones, for that matter—with a sexy man? Not since before they'd thrown all their energies into expanding Clear-Blue Air, at the very least. She hadn't had time for a lunch date, much less the kind of lust-fest she'd enjoyed in her younger years. The kind that lasted for entire weekends and involved not leaving a bed except to grab the kind of sensuous food that could be smeared onto—and eaten off—someone else's hot, naked, sweat-tinged body.

She closed her eyes, her hand clenching tight on the railing. Her heart fluttered in her chest and she tried to make herself move. But she couldn't—not climbing up, but not backing away, either. Not physically, and not in her head.

Was she really considering this? God, she hadn't even looked at the stranger's left hand to make sure he was available. She had no idea if he was actually attracted to her or just an irrepressible flirt. Yet something inside was telling her to take a shot with this man.

It was crazy. Something she'd never considered. Yet right now, at this moment, she was definitely considering it. If he was available…could she do it? Seduce a stranger. Have an anonymous fling, like something out of a blue movie on late-night cable?

She didn't know. All she knew was that the flight to Chicago was a short one so she had to decide quickly. And as she put her foot on the bottom step and began to climb up, Amanda suddenly had to wonder if she was about to embark on the ride of her life.

New Year, New Man!

*For the perfect New Year's punch,
blend the following:*

- *One woman determined to find her inner vixen*
- *A notorious—and notoriously hot!—playboy*
- *A provocative New Year's Eve bash*
- *An impulsive kiss that leads to a night of
explosive passion!*

When the clock hits midnight Claire Daniels
kisses the guy standing closest to her, but
the kiss doesn't end after the bells stop ringing....

Look for

Moonstruck

by *USA TODAY* bestselling author

JULIE KENNER

Available January

---

red-hot reads

www.eHarlequin.com

HB79518

REQUEST YOUR FREE BOOKS!

2 FREE NOVELS PLUS 2 FREE GIFTS!

 Silhouette

ROMANTIC
SUSPENSE

Sparked by Danger, Fueled by Passion.

YES! Please send me 2 FREE Silhouette® Romantic Suspense novels and my 2 FREE gifts (gifts are worth about $10). After receiving them, if I don't wish to receive any more books, I can return the shipping statement marked "cancel." If I don't cancel, I will receive 4 brand-new novels every month and be billed just $4.24 per book in the U.S. or $4.99 per book in Canada. That's a saving of 15% off the cover price! It's quite a bargain! Shipping and handling is just 50¢ per book in the U.S. and 75¢ per book in Canada.* I understand that accepting the 2 free books and gifts places me under no obligation to buy anything. I can always return a shipment and cancel at any time. Even if I never buy another book from Silhouette, the two free books and gifts are mine to keep forever.

240 SDN E39A 340 SDN E39M

Name	(PLEASE PRINT)

Address	Apt. #

City	State/Prov.	Zip/Postal Code

Signature (if under 18, a parent or guardian must sign)

Mail to the **Silhouette Reader Service:**

IN U.S.A.: P.O. Box 1867, Buffalo, NY 14240-1867
IN CANADA: P.O. Box 609, Fort Erie, Ontario L2A 5X3

Not valid for current subscribers to Silhouette Romantic Suspense books.

Want to try two free books from another line?
Call 1-800-873-8635 or visit www.morefreebooks.com.

---

* Terms and prices subject to change without notice. Prices do not include applicable taxes. N.Y. residents add applicable sales tax. Canadian residents will be charged applicable provincial taxes and GST. Offer not valid in Quebec. This offer is limited to one order per household. All orders subject to approval. Credit or debit balances in a customer's account(s) may be offset by any other outstanding balance owed by or to the customer. Please allow 4 to 6 weeks for delivery. Offer available while quantities last.

Your Privacy: Silhouette is committed to protecting your privacy. Our Privacy Policy is available online at www.eHarlequin.com or upon request from the Reader Service. From time to time we make our lists of customers available to reputable third parties who may have a product or service of interest to you. If you would prefer we not share your name and address, please check here. ☐

Help us get it right—We strive for accurate, respectful and relevant communications. To clarify or modify your communication preferences, visit us at www.ReaderService.com/consumerchoice.